T0126378

KILLING AUNTIE

ANDRZEJ BURSA

Translated by
WIESIEK POWAGA

NEW VESSEL PRESS
NEW YORK

KILLING AUNTIE

 New Vessel Press

www.newvesselpress.com

First published in Polish in 1969
by Wydawnictwo Literackie Kraków as *Zabicie ciotki*
Copyright © 2015 Estate of Andrzej Bursa
Translation Copyright © 2015 Wiesiek Powaga

Library of Congress Cataloging-in-Publication Data
Bursa, Andrzej
[Zabicie ciotki. English]
Killing Auntie / Andrzej Bursa; translation by Wiesiek Powaga.
p. cm.
ISBN 978-1-939931-21-4
Library of Congress Control Number 2014947421
I. Poland — Fiction.

REBEL LIT SERIES

Rebel Lit is a new series by New Vessel Press showcasing works of literature that display a spirit of rebellion and challenge. More than merely transgressive, some of these manifest heroism and courage, others walk conspicuously on the wild side; all of the books in the Rebel Lit series are creative works of unusual caliber.

Killing Auntie is the second title in this series. Andrzej Bursa was born in 1932 and died young, at 25, in 1957. Though legend saw fit to attribute his death to suicide, congenital heart disease was what actually brought this startlingly innovative writer to his early end. During his brief lifetime, Bursa wrote poetry and prose in a style that today is instantly recognizable for its bold confrontation with reality through the use of subversion and the absurd. *Killing Auntie* is just that sort of story. Bursa never expected he'd see it published in his lifetime. The senseless violence, the black humor, the collusion of others (though quite humorously recounted) – all these may be read allegorically, as a commentary on the political situation of 1950s Poland, though what comes first is the literary quality itself. Bursa's name became a rallying point for young people all over Poland who wished to express themselves freely, innovatively and without political repercussions.

THANKSGIVING PRAYER (WITH A GRUDGE)

You didn't make me blind
Thank you O Lord

You didn't give me a hump
Thank you O Lord

You didn't make my father an alkie
Thank you O Lord

You didn't give me water on the brain
Thank you O Lord

You didn't make me a stutterer a gimp a midget epileptic
hermaphrodite a horse moss or something from the flora
or fauna
Thank you O Lord

But why did you make me a Pole?

Andrzej Bursa
translated by Wiesiek Powaga

To all who once stood terrified
before the dead perspective of their youth

1

I LEFT HOME AT FOUR IN THE AFTERNOON. AFTER A FEW steps I stopped. I needed a purpose. Nothing came to mind. I resumed my walk like a condemned man, resigned to aimless wandering around the town. I went out for these long and exhausting walks almost every day. But I always made sure I had a purpose. Chores, visits. Never did any of that, of course. After all, I had nothing to do, no one to visit. But the purpose was there, even though I knew it was a sham.

Today for the first time I realized I had no purpose. I went out without a reason. These purposeless, lonely walks were murderous. I knew that. In summer, when I walked through woods, fields or overgrown riverbanks, they at least had some justification. They didn't exhaust me so much. Absorbed into the landscape, becoming part of it, I didn't have to think. I could rest. But in winter the town brought no calm. I ambled around, stopping in front of old archways and shop windows full of cellophane displays but found no solace in either. I appreciated – and understood – the charms of architecture and of the city lights, yet saw no point in contemplating them. I longed for a purpose like a sick man longs for a cure. Held hostage by my own nature, I suffered terribly.

I walked slowly and with difficulty. The downy snow, which had fallen during the day, lay on the pavement like heaps of manna. I waded through them. The interminable circling of the streets was wearing me out. I knew that, overcome by exhaustion, I would soon reach a point when I would think of returning home with pleasure and, bare-

ly standing, rejoice at the sight of my window. But it was
no consolation. I knew too, that back at home, resting on
my bed, I would reach for the mirror and look at myself.
For a long time.

I examined my face several times a day, every day,
looking for signs of maturity, or old age. But the face remained stubbornly young. Nine years of youth lay before
me like an endless fallow field unfit for farming. On top
of that all my limbs were in perfect order and I was in rude
health. There was no salvation. Aimless wandering in bad
weather was no fun. Returning home was impossible. The
thought that I could spend the rest of the afternoon and
the evening poring over reading for my university classes
barred my way. There was only the street, which ruled out
any surprises.

In my wandering I could never keep away from the
center. All the excuses could be found within the surrounding boulevards. Today I hadn't dared to break my
habit. Yet the main streets and squares tired me with their
noise and crowds. I turned surreptitiously into a narrow,
almost empty street close to the main thoroughfare. I
found myself in the middle of a labyrinth of old streets
bordering on the center yet completely isolated from it.
Bells hung on wires by the gates. There was snow on the
backs of the crabs, unicorns and little bears carved over
the pediments. The labyrinth wasn't big. I could cross it
both ways in ten minutes. So I walked as slowly as I could,
trying to keep my strides short, resisting the temptation to
stop. I reached the stone wall of the Capuchin monastery.
I knew that in a few seconds I'd come to a small square by
the river. From there I could see the paved alley that I'd
have to take as my return route. The prospect made me
want to stop several times and run the other way. But the
route led through the streets I knew by heart; there was no
point in running away from the tarmac alley straight back
into the embrace of a noisy road.

When I got to the end of the wall I stopped for a moment's rest, like a swimmer about to plunge back into the water. I looked to one side. Two stone angels wearing snowy hats stood guarding the small gate in front of a church. The courtyard before the little church was an oasis of peace. Over the surrounding wall, below street level, tree branches from the orchard on the other side were sticking out. They were covered in snow. I was long hardened to all kinds of soppiness and so was able to look calmly at the relief on the walls and the trees growing in the cloister, which I had known so well since childhood.

From the door leading into the enclosure a bearded monk came out with a broad wooden shovel and began to clear the snow. He didn't pay any attention to me but I felt awkward. I stepped out of his way and began to study the relief on the wall. The monk kept shoveling the snow, panting laboriously. The longer we were alone the more awkward I felt. In the end I reached the point of no return. Slowly, I approached the gate and entered the church. I took a quiet pew at the back. I was not alone. Three elderly women knelt in front of me, two in the pew, one on the stone floor. Above the altar flickered a little flame like a small red heart. Next to the side altar shone a luminous entrance to a small cavern. Inside it, behind a strong grille, lay the golden arm of a seventeenth century hero.

Once, I knew the legend well about the hero who bequeathed his golden arm, a gift from the king, to the Capuchin order. Today some details were missing from my memory. Hiding in the pew I took the role of an observer. A banal and thankless role: there was nothing to observe here. From the sacristy emerged a surpliced monk with a stole over his neck. Briskly, he crossed the floor and shut himself in the confessional. I didn't see his face clearly but with a beard and a high brow he seemed to me beautiful. He was tall, broad-shouldered, not young. The trellis on the confessional door closed, the stole was hung outside.

I thought that at this hour it was unlikely anyone would come to confession. By the altar I spotted the same monk who'd been sweeping the snow. He was performing some strange ritual that involved a lot of kneeling. It was high time for me to leave; I just didn't feel like it. In the empty church (the three women being gone), facing the mute expectation of the priest-confessor, I felt I had found my role. I got up and walked up to the confessional, knelt and knocked. For a fleeting moment I felt fear and stage fright but didn't back down. Something rustled inside the confessional and the priest welcomed me with a Latin formula. I took a deep breath and recited back:

"I last came to confession more or less six – no – seven years ago."

"Why so long, my son?"

"I lost faith."

"What else, my son?"

The priest's voice was weary and passionless. My blasphemous confession didn't make much impression on him. I was crestfallen. I hesitated. I didn't know what to say. Desperately I was trying to remember the formulae from school confessions.

"Since then ... since then I offended the Lord with many sins ..."

"Confess them, my son."

"I was ..." I hesitated again, "I was disobedient with my superiors ... I lied, and then bore false witness against my brother ..."

I was getting hopelessly confused.

"What else, my son?"

I frowned and after some thought whispered triumphantly:

"I sinned against the sixth commandment."

The priest stirred in his seat.

"Many times?"

"Oh, no, not that many," I sighed regretfully.

"What else, my son?"

I couldn't sense any concern in my confessor's voice. Feverishly I was looking for words with which I could reveal to him the full horror of my inner life, which should terrify a holy man. In vain. The priest was already whispering the final formula. In a moment I would hear him knock on the confessional and walk away defeated. I quickly pressed my lips to the wooden lattice and whispered earnestly:

"Father ... Holy Father," I corrected myself, "I concealed one sin."

The priest leaned to the lattice. I lowered my voice.

"I concealed a terrible sin ..." I went for a dramatic pause and then whispered emphatically:

"I killed a human being."

Ah, no more indifferent "What else, my son?" now. The priest was panting. After a moment's silence he asked in an unnaturally loud voice:

"Whom?"

"My aunt."

"Oh, my son ... It's a terrible sin, terrible ..."

The priest was lost for words. Now that he was lost for words I was cold and to the point.

"How did it happen?"

In the priest's voice, apart from a hellish, almost unchristian curiosity, I detected a note of enthusiasm.

"Holy Father," I whispered gravely, "'tis unfitting to speak about."

"In confession one must tell everything, everything," he insisted pleadingly.

I decided to be succinct.

"Ok, then. I killed her with a hammer."

"A hammer ... Oh my son, it's a terrible sin, a grave sin ..."

"Holy Father, more important than the gate of Hades is my soul," I replied courteously.

The priest fell silent for a while and then asked:

"Had your aunt wronged you in any way?"

"No."

"So why did you kill her?"

I hung my head.

"Were you led to it by the repulsive jingle of gold?"

The priest was trying to rise to his role. I felt grateful.

"No, Father, to the contrary."

"Why to the contrary?"

"Killing my aunt, I deprived myself of my main means of support. She gave me board and lodging."

"So why did you do it?"

"I'm a murderer, Father."

The priest fell silent again. And after a while:

"How old are you, my son?"

"Twenty-one."

"Oh, twenty-one ... Was it ... was it your first time?"

"First time what, Father?"

"Had you killed before?"

"No, Father. I would have confessed, wouldn't I?"

"True. Oh, my son, repent your deed and cry over your soul."

"I can't repent, Father."

"Why, my son?"

"I'm a hardened sinner."

"Oh, my son ..." The priest was hopelessly confused. "Oh, my son, cry over your soul..."

Curiosity won the upper hand.

"But you had to have a motive. Why did you kill?"

"I don't know, Father."

He hesitated.

"You are not ... sick, are you?"

"No, Father."

"Then why, my son? Why?"

"I sought peace in crime."

"You can find peace only in prayer."

"I'm too young to waste my days on prayers."

"But, son ..." the priest was irritated. "There are so many other sins ..." He stopped abruptly. After a while he started again: "Are you feeling weak and abandoned?"

"Oh, I am, Father."

"Then repent your sin and cry with me. Difficult years of prison, provided you spend them in remorse and penitence, will atone for your crime."

"I've no intention of going to prison."

"How have you managed to hide your crime?"

"I haven't. I've done it only this morning."

"What have you done with the corpse?"

"For now it's in my kitchen. I'll try to get rid of it."

"How ..." He bit his tongue, apparently realizing the question was not quite in keeping with his work as a confessor.

"I've got a plan."

"I don't want to know. Do you repent of your sin, my son?"

"I can't, Father."

"Repent, my son," he pleaded with me tearfully. "Or you'll go to hell."

"Is it horrible, Father?"

"Oh, son!" the priest cried, grateful for my question.

And he began to paint the picture. The way he did it told me he was just a catechist. But his picture of hell surpassed all the best religion lessons I could remember from childhood. My confessor was inspired. Throughout his life he had been unleashing the horrors of hell to scare small-time sinners for their pranks played on teachers, for masturbation or laziness, to have his efforts rewarded with today's confession. The grand vision of inferno painted for the benefit of such an extraordinary criminal was the sweet fruit that fell into his lap in an empty church, out of the blue, on an afternoon one could expect nothing from. Necessity breeds inventors, necessity breeds heroes. Today I learned that necessity – or rather need – breeds artists. I had seen many reproductions of Old Masters depicting hell but none had come close to my confessor's tirade. That was real hell. Seething, blazing, putrid. I easily forgave my confessor some catechetical naïveté for the sweeping power of his vision.

The church was empty again. The monk had put out all the lights except for the little red lamp. There were only two of us, the hero's golden arm and hell. At last the priest ran out of breath.

"My son," he pleaded, "repent your crime."

"I can't, Father."

"Then I can't give you absolution."

It all began to turn nasty.

"Then I'll walk away with hell in my heart."

I got on my feet, as if ready to leave. The priest rustled hurriedly inside the confessional.

"No, son, don't go away." He lowered his voice and I heard in his words a playful note.

"If you can't find in yourself perfect remorse, the most pleasing to the Lord, then imperfect remorse will be enough … Think of all the horrors of hell, and fear the deed that condemns you to such torture. That will be enough."

The priest's voice was so sympathetic I was ready to express my imperfect remorse. Still, I held back. Showing imperfect remorse would give my confessor paltry satisfaction. This extraordinary confession would have a very cheap and trivial epilogue in a common criminal's fear of chains and fire. So I said:

"Father, imperfect remorse will not atone for such a crime before the Lord."

The priest was delighted.

"My son," he said, "words like these suffice for remorse."

"It's not worth much, though."

"Son, I am crying for your soul," whispered the priest, "I truly am."

He felt his inspiration was waning but still could not let go of me. The confession got stuck in a dead end. I pitied the priest. Anxiously, I started looking for a way out of the impasse. In the end I suggested:

"My crime is still fresh today. I'm still breathing blood. But tomorrow, or in a few days' time, if God lets me live that long, perhaps the grace of remorse will come to me."

"Come tomorrow then, my son," hurriedly advised the priest. "In the afternoon or evening. Between four and six. I will wait for you every day."

The priest was excited and joyous. He appreciated the chance I gave him. Today's confession would be more than just a beautiful moment in his life. It would open a difficult, glorious path to the salvation of a murderer, a path full of terrible mysteries. I had elevated my cleric to the level of a missionary converting cannibals, of a Saint Hieronymus taming a lion. He was pleased like a child, and it pleased me too. When I rose from my knees, the priest reminded me once more:

"Well then, between four and six, four and six in the evening."

His voice trembled with the anxiety of a parting lover.

2

EVERY TIME I OPENED MY EYES IN THE MORNING AUNTIE was already on her feet. Humming in her low alto voice, she bustled around the stove, preparing our breakfast. The simplicity and good nature of this woman was too much of an everyday occurrence to make any impression on me. Nevertheless, from time to time, there were moments it moved me, though more often recently it irritated me. Auntie earned her living as a sort of middleman in the local wool trade or some such business; I was never really interested in that. She worked like a dog.

Apart from myself, a twenty-one-year-old loafer, Auntie also provided for her old mother and her crippled sister. Both lived in a remote small town in the mountains. They visited us more than four times a year. I hated those visits. When Granny, wrapped up in black frocks, her ears all smeared with some white pasty medicine, sat at the table, it was revolting. I felt even more disgust toward her daughter – a young apathetic hunchback with coke-bottle spectacles. They were both very devout and crossed themselves eagerly before every dish. Auntie, once a beautiful and worldly woman, with them suddenly remembered which church she belonged to. The dinners were better then, and that was the only upside to those visits.

Auntie maintained that she would like to have her old mother and her crippled sister live with her but it was impossible because our flat was just too small. And she had to keep her eye on me while I was studying. It wasn't true. I have no doubt she preferred to share the flat with her favorite nephew than with her half-dead mother and blockhead sister. I was the only person Auntie truly loved. She liked it when I whistled during my morning shave in the bathroom, or polished off her scrambled eggs with gusto. She knew I had to finish my studies and she spared no effort making sure I did. However, there was a limit to how much effort she could spare, and that limit was not far off.

Auntie had reached the point when she needed quiet recuperation before the terminal advance of old age. And yet still she worked like a horse. She carried big packs of merchandise, went on business trips, often sleeping on the train. She paid for it with her heart, her liver, varicose veins. She was trying to cure them, visiting doctors and following their orders. But often life made this impractical. So Auntie suffered on, now and again letting out with a groan or a sigh, and who knows — perhaps that was the cause of the whole affair. Normally she bore her illnesses and old age with gallant heroism. She took care of herself, was not above a discreet touch of makeup and generally kept her spirits up, waking me up almost every morning with a joke. Truly, when I look back at those times, I have to admit she was indeed a very, very good woman.

Certainly, the cause of this whole situation could not lay in the small misunderstandings that naturally took place between us. In fact, if I remember correctly, no such incidents occurred that day. It was March, the frost still held fast. Auntie had to breathe on the windowpane to check the temperature on the outside thermometer. It was about ten o'clock. The snow glistened on the metal windowsill. But inside the room it was actually warm. I remember that when I was putting my slippers on, Auntie made some chirpy remark, which irritated me. Without hurrying things, I put on my trousers, a shirt and a sweater. I ate my breakfast of scrambled eggs, bread and tea with appetite. Auntie asked me what time my lectures began, to which I replied that they started at ten and therefore I had plenty of time. After breakfast Auntie asked me to hammer a nail into the wall so she could hang a mirror. This new task gave me a certain satisfaction. The hammer especially proved to be an oddly pleasant tool to handle, something I had not paid any attention to before. When the nail was hammered in, and I sat sprawling lazily on the stool, I was still holding the hammer in my hands. I was playing with it.

Auntie was getting ready to go out. She looked into the room, opened and closed the sideboard, checked the gas and bent down to pull on her boots. Then I walked up to her from behind and with all my strength I whacked her twice on the side of the head.

There was no doubt Auntie was a corpse. She lay still, a small trickle of blood pouring out of god knows where, as there was no visible wound. I grabbed her by the shoulders and turned her face up. No, there was no doubt – she was a corpse.

"Corpse," I pronounced half out loud. "Corpse, corpse, corpse …" I sort of sang to myself, and felt uneasy.

Auntie's eyes were opened wide; her moist teeth peered out from behind parted lips. And the blood – from her nose, mouth, ears – flowing in tiny rivulets into puddles on the floor. This fleshy, ripened body ceased to be fifty-four years old, ceased to feel pain, suffer illnesses, to enjoy itself. The shapely though overworked hands were now wooden. This body was so alien to me that I found it impossible at that moment to feel any pity or regret.

I became a little nauseous. I went back to my room and lay on the bed. I felt my hand sticking to the sheets. It turned out that both hands had blood on them; god knows how it happened, as there wasn't really that much blood, and I hadn't been touching it. So I went to the bathroom. It angered me to see I was leaving bloody marks on the tap. It struck me as too literary. Washing my hands, all the time I felt in my stomach and in my throat the morning's breakfast: sweet tea and peppery scrambled eggs. And before me – Auntie's corpse. I bent over the toilet bowl, pushed two fingers down my throat and vomited. After I threw it all up, once more I thoroughly washed my hands, rinsed my mouth and drank some water. Then carefully examined my face in the mirror.

I looked bad, but that could be put down to vomiting. At any rate, I saw in myself nothing of a murderer. I still had the same lock of hair on my forehead, lips, nose and the gray good-natured eyes of a luckless boy who at twenty-one was still just an awkward teenager. I took out a cigarette and smoking, walked to the kitchen, where I sat over Auntie's corpse. As I smoked the fear began to rise. It was making me sweat. I was cold and nauseated. My fingers, by now burned by the cigarette, seemed so weak and helpless I could hardly believe what they had been capable of.

And yet they were capable. I felt pride, which alas was immediately soured by icy, slimy fear. It seemed there was nothing left for me but to go down and make a report at the police station, or simply stop the first policeman in the street and bring him in here. The policeman: red face of the common man, matter-of-fact, unbelieving tone – I was gripped by spasms of terror. I dragged myself back to bed and tried to calm down. I was talking to myself in a half-voice, as any fully spoken sentence would have been drowned out by the pounding fear.

"Calm down, my boy, calm down … Everything will be all right. We'll manage … Ha ha, we will …" Something broke loose inside me. "Never mind, it's nothing. I know it sounds paradoxical. Never mind, it's nothing. You'll live … We'll get out of it … Remember," I raised my finger, "you're twenty-one years old. You have to live. Your whole life is ahead of you. Women, travel, work, adventures. You are twenty-one years old. Twenty-one. You are young, young ..."

I was telling myself this and believed it all, though I did not at all feel twenty-one years old, let alone that it was a good reason I should live, and pleasantly at that. This does not mean I felt physically weak. I could have gotten up and lifted that heavy chair off the floor with my left hand. But why? What for? Don't move, calm down.

I looked at my watch. It was ten o'clock. I still could make it to the lecture. The thought of getting out of the flat filled me with energy. I put my boots on, but as soon as I laced them up I changed my mind. This special day called for some little celebration. Devil knows why I thought that by turning up at the lecture I might be tempting fate. I unlaced my old skiing boots, took them off and put on my slippers again. I carried out these small tasks with precision and diligence. I was terrified but my movements were calm now. I began to consider ways of disposing of the corpse. It seemed child's play. I'd chop the body up, flush some parts down the loo, burn some, take others away in parcels and throw them in the river or bury them. Bury them where? Ah, it's a trifle. I know a quiet place in the woods on the outskirts of town.

I felt light-headed and carefree. I decided to carry out the plan without further ado. I went into the kitchen with an open penknife. I started with a finger. It turned out to be not that simple. The blade was blunt, the flesh gave in with difficulty, chafing and tearing. The bone just would not cut. I put away the penknife and fetched an axe. I swung it and the finger sprang off. Meanwhile, the tip of the thumb struck me in the eye. I picked up the finger and dropped it down the toilet bowl. It floated in the yellowish water like a pale sausage. I flushed the loo. The water gushed, snatched the finger and sucked it into the black void, but after a while the finger floated back to the surface. I yanked the chain. The pipes rumbled deeply, the water rose and filled the bowl. The finger disappeared.

I took a piss. The finger resurfaced. The water subsided slowly. I fished out the wet finger and held it hopelessly between my own two fingers.

Apparently, that was not the way. It became clear to me that disposing of this hefty, one hundred and fifty pound body, depriving it of its full, overripe figure and its bale of fresh skin was not going to be as easy as it seemed to me, fed on the literature from the "time of contempt." The corpse defended its individuality, its natural right to biological decay. Somewhat embarrassed, I returned to the kitchen and laid the hacked-off finger on Auntie's breast.

There was something of a gesture of reconciliation in that.

3

Around midday I went out. The street was freezing cold, hostile. The sun, which in the morning lit the snow on the windowsill so beautifully, had disappeared. It was gray and cold. I felt hungry. Up till now, Auntie had cooked lunch at home. If she was away I ate at any old place. I stepped into a third-rate bar on the corner. It was full. There was one free table in the middle of the room but I retreated. Sweaty, yellow-brown lacquered walls, stuffy stench of the room, trivial faces of the eaters – all that disgusted me. I walked on. I was approaching the town center when it came to mind that a day like this could be honored with a good meal at a first-rate restaurant.

In the window an enormous salmon on a bed of red caviar lay in a wreath of parsley. From behind the matted glass peered lush leaves of exotic plants, creating the impression of a perfect refuge from the freezing street. I pushed the door open and headed for the cloakroom. The cloakroom lady was very tall and very big. Much bigger than Auntie. I assessed her at some hundred and seventy-five pounds and thanked god it wasn't her corpse I had in my flat. I was about to unbutton my coat when I saw the waiter standing at the entrance to the room. The waiter was a black-haired man of about thirty-five. Dressed in routine waiter's garb: slightly wide black trousers, white apron, white shirt. He was playing with a napkin, looking in my direction. I felt I was afraid of waiters. At that moment I thought of one thing only: avoid a situation where he could come near me and say something. I walked back to the cloakroom lady.

"Can I make a phone call?"

Straight away I realized what a stupid idea that was; I could have asked for a pack of cigarettes, even those expensive ones, foreign, which could not be gotten anywhere else. But it was too late. I picked up the receiver and under the cloakroom lady's unfriendly gaze I dialed a fictitious number, which nevertheless began with a five, like all other telephone numbers in our town. I heard a woman's voice.

"Hello," I said calmly. "May I speak to Andrzej, please?"

When told "Wrong number," I apologized and thanked the woman sincerely.

Back on the street I was hit by sharp wind. I thought of my flat and happily turned toward home. Home sweet home. When at last I reached home, still dressed, in my coat and hat, I looked into the kitchen.

Auntie had not changed, except for the blood around her and on her face, which had dried into a blackish, brown scab. I took my coat off and, smoking a cigarette, I began to devise a plan of action. Without question, I had to remove the corpse from the kitchen and make some lunch. The gas was weak so I decided to light a fire under the kitchen stove and cook myself a proper meal. In the sideboard I found a couple of red cutlets, bread, frankfurters, butter, eggs and potatoes in a basket. There was also tea and even a bottle of Hungarian wine, which Auntie must have hidden there for some special occasion.

I started peeling the potatoes. I was no good at it. Until now I hardly ever peeled potatoes. Auntie always prepared our meals and I helped only when my manly strength or my manly height was called for. By the second potato I cut my finger. The wound was not big but deep and bled profusely. Clumsily pulling up the shirtsleeve with my other, healthy but dirty hand, I ran to the sink. The tiny wound hit by a stream of cold water began to smart. I put my finger into my mouth and sucked it. The pain abated but every time I took the finger out of my mouth, the pale, barely visible slit began to fill with scarlet blood. I went to the cupboard with the first aid kit and rummaged through it, finding some gauze, bandages and iodine. There was no other disinfectant. It took me a long time before I managed to dress my wound and tie a nice tight knot on the finger.

I sat at the kitchen table miserable and worn out, nursing my wounded finger in my fist. Hunger and cigarettes pressed on my brain like a heavy gray substance. I had no strength left to finish peeling the potatoes. I'd have frankfurters with scrambled eggs and bread. Absentmindedly I dragged myself to the sideboard to fetch a saucepan. Suddenly something tripped me up. I struggled to keep my balance and, desperately clutching at anything, I banged my head right against the edge of the sideboard.

"Fuck!" I cursed, loudly and angrily.

The object that tripped me up was Auntie's corpse. Overwhelming pain paralyzed me briefly. Yet hungry and exhausted, I found in me new layers of strength. I was able to refrain from ignobly taking it out on the inanimate object that had caused me pain. The cause of my frustration had to be pacified so that in the future similar accidents could be avoided. I went about it with blunt angry assiduousness. I wrapped my hands under Auntie's shoulders and lifted her. She was very heavy. As I pulled her along I smelled an unpleasant odor coming out of her open mouth. I turned my face away. Suddenly I felt the body putting up an insurmountable resistance. I pulled with all my strength but it would not budge. It turned out Auntie's foot was hooked around one of the sideboard's legs. I had to lay her down and unhook the damn foot. I tried a different hold. I grabbed her by the wrists and began pulling her across the floor. This was not easy either. The hands were stiff, unwieldy and difficult to steer with. Still, I managed to gain some ground. After a while her head hit the threshold. The first part of the job was behind us. Now I raised the head, then the shoulders, and pulled them over the threshold.

The hallway was narrow and cluttered. The bathroom door was hung in such a way that the body had to be turned around 180 degrees. This required a well thought-out plan and precise execution. First thing to do was remove all possible objects that stood in the way of the body. So I took down the bowl from the small chest standing by the wall, then the box full of wool, and put them away. Then, with some effort, I lifted the chest and put that away too. Slowly, I was forgetting my hunger and fatigue. I felt good, like with any noble manual labor, not the perfunctory kind but labor requiring a creative element. Bit by bit, carefully, I was pushing the corpse over the threshold, trying to position it so that in a minute I could easily pull it inside the bathroom. Now and again I spoke to myself, giving myself warnings, praises, reprimands and words of encouragement:

"Well done. Yes ... No, no, no, we won't get anywhere this way. Wait ... Wait, my friend. Now. Yes, that's it. See?"

Suddenly the doorbell rang. The sharp, short sound cut through the soft shuffle of my work and my effortful panting. Crouching by the corpse, I froze. I held my breath. The floorboards at the opposite end of the hallway creaked gently. I remembered that Mazan, a fellow student from my year, was to visit me today. Always with his nose in the books. At the same time it crossed my mind that the room was dark and the kitchen windows faced the courtyard, so the light should not betray me. I realized all this very quickly and the intruder soon began to bore and irritate me. I was not scared at all; he was simply disturbing me. Mazan rang the doorbell again, waited a bit ... then tried knocking. Then the door rattled and I heard something like muffled rapping and scraping. Mazan was writing me a note. Finally he finished writing and walked away with a loud clank of his skiing boots, which I somehow missed when he first arrived. I was very tempted to read his note. After waiting a good while, I quietly opened the door and picked the note up off the floor. "Jurek, I came to see you at 6. Come to the lectures tomorrow, we'll need you. Ciao. Tadek."

"Ah, there we are," I said aloud. "There we are ..."

This was just what I expected. And I was not disappointed. I knew too what they would need me for. My friends were organizing tea with dancing, and wanted me to help. I couldn't care less, but I couldn't afford not to get involved.

I returned to my work. Pulling the corpse into the bathroom turned out to be easier than expected. Loading it into the bath was not so easy. The body was falling through my hands, resisting me. Now the head, now the feet knocked against the floor tiles. At long last I managed to fit it in. The legs stuck up in the air and the skirt slipped halfway down the thighs. Automatically I pulled it over the knees, only to realize the pointlessness of the gesture, as sooner or later I would have to strip the corpse naked anyway. I found the prospect rather embarrassing. I had never seen Auntie naked. Only once, in passing, I'd seen her bare buttocks, and for the rest of the day felt weird in her company.

I returned to the kitchen and on the gas stove made scrambled eggs, which I covered with cold frankfurters and bread. Luckily, by now the gas was working better.

4

IN THE MORNING I WOKE UP FRESH AND RESTED. I JUMPED out of bed and did a few vaguely gymnastic exercises. The room was a bit chilly, I had an appetite, good humor and felt very young. Auntie's canary sent off a peel of brilliant trills from his cage:

"Tru – tiu – tu …"

I echoed him:

"Tiu – tiu … Good morning, little birdie. Good morning, Cracow, good morning, sun … Good morning, good morning!"

I ran to fetch a bag with seeds and served the birdie a copious spoonful in his bowl. The wall glittered with playful sun bunnies. It was cold outside but warmer than yesterday. The thermometer was showing twenty degrees. It was 8:20 am. Phew, at last I had had a good night's sleep. I had slept almost ten hours. Now I felt rested, strong, young and independent. Whistling, I ran to the bathroom. I would have loved a bath but unfortunately the bathtub was filled with the corpse.

I stood in front of the mirror.

"Good morning, Jurek," I smiled. "Hello, Jerzy."

I ran the tap and washed myself from the waist up.

"Good morning, Auntie," I turned towards the bath.

"How did my love
sleep in the tub?"

I was singing, crying and shaking off the cold water. After drying myself with a thick hairy towel, I started to shave. I was a bit cold but didn't put my shirt on, showing off instead my arms and shoulders, perhaps still rather boyish for my age. As I dressed, I did gymnastics the whole time, and hummed to myself.

I put the kettle on the stove and started preparing breakfast. Once more I considered my situation. It was not bad. I was confident, but without the easy optimism which had momentarily swept over me immediately after killing Auntie. I was aware now that disposing of the corpse would require a long effort but I believed I was up to it. Auntie's sudden disappearance should not arouse any suspicions from the neighbors or friends. She often went away without any warning and could even be absent for several days at a time. I decided that after ten days – during which time I should certainly manage to get rid of the corpse – I would start a search. First I would write to Granny, then to friends and Auntie's business associates in other towns, and finally I would place an ad in the press and call the police.

The food in the larder would last me only two or three days. After breakfast I searched the flat for money. In Auntie's handbag, in the linen cupboard between the sheets and in the drawer of her night table I found bills totaling one thousand and seven hundred zlotys. That would tide me over for now. Later I might sell Auntie's clothes and her jewelry: her wedding ring, the ruby ring and the small necklace. Apart from that, inside the corpse's mouth I would find a gold bridge, though I should probably wait a bit before selling it. At any rate, I'd be financially secure for a few months. Then it would be summer, I could go off on a camping trip, and in my last year at university I'd find a job.

I already started thinking of finding suitable, not-too-absorbing employment. But first things first – I had to get cracking with disposing of the corpse. I knew I couldn't do it in one go, that the job had to be spread over several days and that I would have to be extremely careful. It crossed my mind that I could burn part of the body in the stove. Frequent trips with packages containing bits of the corpse struck me as too risky.

The lectures started in the afternoon. So I decided to get on with it now. What I could not decide on was whether to light the kitchen stove or the one in the bedroom. Eventually I settled on both. The flat was pretty cold. Although I sleep and spend most of my time in the room, recently I'd come to like sitting around the kitchen. Perhaps it was that silly power which brings the murderer to the scene of his crime, which one reads so much about in novels. Of course I did not feel like a murderer. Killing Auntie was in my case the result of so many interlocking mental states, of complexes and depression that I had analyzed and digested so many times before, and analyzing and digesting them all over again would have been only another pointless routine. In fact, my engagement with the corpse ruled out in advance any element of remorse, if I'd had any in the first place. The corpse was simply my partner in a hazardous game, in which admittedly I couldn't win anything, but on the other hand could lose my life. I even had a kind of respect for the corpse, the way one usually does for a strong opponent.

I had a bit of stage fright before lighting the stove. It was a much more difficult task than peeling potatoes. I tried not to admit it to myself though. With a poker and a coal spade I swept out the ash, revealing the bare grate. Quite a large proportion of the ash missed the bucket and ended up on the floor. But I didn't worry too much about it. The floor needed to be scrubbed anyway. It had small puddles of Auntie's dried-up blood on it, as well as a few drops of mine from the unfortunate finger. I thought I would have to wash the shirt too; its sleeves were stained with blood from when I was trying to bandage my wound. Taking bloodied linen to a laundry would be rather risky in my situation.

I placed a few sheets of old newspaper on the grate, and on top of them a few dry splinters of wood. Only then I decided to place among all this flammable material some pieces of coal. The first match went out the moment I brought it near the stove. The second and the third likewise. I remembered that there was a draft inside the stove that put out small flames. I hit on the idea of lighting a piece of paper outside the stove and putting it inside only when it was properly burning. Alas, I ran out of matches. I looked on top of the stove; I found several boxes, all empty. A search of the entire flat was equally fruitless. I was delighted when on Auntie's night table I found a box which was heavy and rattled when I picked it up. But all the matches inside were burned. There was no other way: I had to go downstairs and buy matches. I accepted it without grumbling.

I had to go out to buy cigarettes anyway, of which I had only two left; they wouldn't last me till midday. In the kiosk on the corner I purchased two boxes of matches – one for my pocket, the other for the household – a packet of cigarettes and today's paper.

I could not refuse myself the pleasure of leafing through the pages before lighting the stove. I sat on the stool and checked the headlines. I always started with news reports, although the names of diplomats or international events did not interest me at all. Inside there was an article with an enticing title but the text was so long and gray I knew I would never be able to read it. Below I found a column in italics signed by a local hack, from whom I couldn't expect anything good. Finally I reached the back page, my favorite. Among the gossip, small ads, weather forecasts and other short pieces I found the following headline: "Matricide on Death Row."

I read on:

"The trial concluded yesterday of Edward Wąsacz,

aged nineteen, from the village Żylin, in Dąbrowa district, accused of carrying out murder on the person of his mother, Weronika Wąsacz, aged forty-five. On the 27th of this month the accused returned home in a state of inebriation and when his mother remonstrated with him he punched her in the face. The woman began to scream and cry for help, in response to which her son struck her on the head with an axe, causing an open fracture of the skull. Following this, the murderer buried the victim's body under a pile of manure in the yard. Thanks to an energetic investigation the perpetrator was arrested just forty-eight hours later. After a guilty verdict in the county court, the pathological killer was sentenced to death."

I found no parallel between this piece of news and my current situation. There was absolutely no psychological similarity between me and the country bumpkin from the Dąbrowa district. Nevertheless, I read the column carefully several times. I smiled to myself, imagining the sly drunk burying his corpse in a pile of manure. I also calculated how long forty-eight hours was, and whether it had passed since my killing of Auntie. It turned out it had not.

"Good," I said aloud and kneeled before the stove, matches in hand.

I lit a sheet of newspaper and threw it inside. It curled up in flames and fell on the coal in a charred, scrunched up lump. The stove was black and cold again. I lit another sheet and placed it in such a way as to direct the flames onto the dry wood, then quickly put the burning match to the papers that were already there from earlier. The flame rose clear and high. The wood began to burn. Triumphantly I closed the stove hatch. A playful bright light flickered through the long slits in the iron hatch. Alas, it started to weaken and soon the stove gaped at me with empty eye sockets. It died. I was annoyed. I stuffed in as much paper as the stove would take and went to the larder, where Auntie kept a bottle of kerosene; there was still some left at the bottom. I lit the paper and poured the kerosene on the feeble flame. The inside of the stove burst into light and everything went up in flames in a jiffy. I watched as the wood caught fire and how the flame cuddled up to the coal with little sparks and made it glow.

I loved fire. As a child I could spend hours watching the charming yet fleeting shapes of burning objects, their last slow throes before annihilation. I liked watching old newspapers and trash transmogrify in their last moments into burning craters, assuming blindingly white forms. I liked watching the miraculous transformation of frail dry flakes now crackling in scarlet opulence. A few prods with the poker inside the stove stirred up a golden blizzard. I put some more pieces of coal in and closed the hatch.

It was much nicer in the kitchen now. Of course, the freshly kindled fire could not yet give much warmth but I knew it would soon be warm. I put a saucepan of water on the range and got busy with lunch. I fortified my tea with the Hungarian wine and checked the stove. Most of the coal was now glowing red. I took some of the glowing embers on the pan and carried them to the stove in the bedroom. Then I stoked both stoves with more coal. I felt like a prince in my modest castle. I looked into the pantry to compose a menu for the lunch. First of all the cutlets, which had been lying on the shelf for two days. I would fry them with potatoes. Fried eggs would make an excellent side dish too. Some sort of soup crossed my mind but I dismissed it as too complicated. I put on a big kettle of water. I checked for sugar in the sugar bowl and it turned out there was plenty. I spread the newspaper on the floor, brought in the basket, took out the knife and began peeling potatoes. It wasn't difficult at all. I worked slowly, unhurriedly, calmly. Just as I finished the third potato, I felt a pang of anxiety. I felt vaguely as if I had committed a kind of desertion. It was all too pretty, too pastoral.

After all, with all this calm and confidence one must not forget that there was a corpse nearby. And it could cause trouble. One silly accident and the crime would be out. I checked the stove. The heat was wonderful. I pushed the potatoes aside and went over to the bathroom.

When I stood over the corpse, I had to reprimand myself again for being absentminded and impulsive. I had brought no tools with me. I returned to the kitchen to fetch the axe. But with the axe I stood over the corpse just as helpless as before. The corpse was lying on the bottom of the tub, which precluded any sensible chop. I could of course hack at its face, open up the stomach or cut the chest, but that would not advance the job in any real way. My eyes alighted on the feet, sticking up above the edge of the bath. Why not start with the legs? I took a good swing and struck, aiming more or less in the middle of the tibia between the foot and the knee, at the point where the leg was resting on the rim of the bath. I struck and the bathroom was filled with a deep metallic boom. The bath rang out like a bell. I'd missed. I'd only scratched the calf, tearing up the stocking and the skin, and making a dent in the bath. The boom seemed interminable. I heard it out patiently, feeling terribly guilty. When the boom died out I tapped myself on the forehead.

"Think, man. Think. Chopping off legs with an axe makes no sense whatsoever," I explained to myself. "And it's equally pointless chopping them off here. Rather, you should try for smaller pieces, ready to be put in the stove. And finally, there's no point in chopping at legs that are still dressed in stockings and shoes."

So I unlaced the shoes, pulled them off the dead feet and stood them at attention in front of Auntie's bed. Then I pulled up the skirt and unclasped the stockings. I rolled them up into a ball and threw them in the stove. From the larder I fetched a small and rather blunt saw. I positioned myself and had a first go. It wasn't too bad. I

realized that resting my hand just above the corpse's knee
I could saw the leg into pieces any size I liked, just like
they do it in the country when they saw birch branches
that go straight in the stove. So first, I had to disconnect
the foot. I cleared my throat to emphasize the gravity of
the work, and began:

Shrrt-Shrrt ... shrrt-shrrt ... shrrt-shrrrt ...

On the whole, I was making good progress. Several
times the saw jumped out of the groove and scratched the
skin, but that is to be expected during sawing.

Shrrt-Shrrt ... shrrt-shrrt ... shrrt-shrrrt ...

I got to the bone, which proved tougher, but then it
started to give way, too. Then the saw blade got stuck in
some sticky muck. I wiped it off with a finger and flicked
the gunge into the loo, then got on with the sawing again.
Muscles, tendons, bones – everything gave way. My confidence grew. It turns out I am not all thumbs, as Auntie
used to tell me. I smiled at the joke, which came to my
mind unbidden. When the foot was nearly cut through
I put away the saw and reached for the axe. With a few
brisk chops I finally severed it from the leg. Stupidly
though, I wasn't holding it, and the foot plopped into
the toilet bowl. I cursed and delicately fished it out with
two fingers. For a moment I hesitated whether I should
wipe it dry so as not put a wet item in the stove, and even
made a movement toward the towel, but laughed aloud
at myself. I put the foot on the hot range in the kitchen
and returned to sawing off another piece of leg. This time
I was careful to avoid the embarrassment with the toilet
bowl. At long last the foot and the other piece lay in front
of the stove.

The heat inside the stove was wonderful. I threw in
more pieces of paper and wood to build up the fire and
chucked the foot into the shimmering void. It sizzled. I
heard a hollow thump of the falling weight. The flames
began to lick the new item. The skin began to blush and

stretch. I smelled the odor of burning tallow. I was very tempted to watch the struggle of the flames with the corpse's foot a bit longer, but overcame the temptation and closed the hatch. It could have led to some kind of unhealthy sadism, which so far had been absent in my relationship with the corpse. Anyway, the fire burned better with the hatch shut.

Somehow I lost interest in preparing the cutlets now. There was still time, I told myself. And went to the room and lay on the bed. Like an old sybarite I took time to arrange the pillows under my head and shoulders, and to wrap myself in the blanket. I wanted to make my bed as soft and comfortable as possible. I reached out for a book. Oddly, it happened to be Dante's *Inferno*. I was irked by this theatricality, which from time to time emerged against my will and against – I was very much aware of that – my actual situation. But then, what was I to do if this was the only book within the range of my hand? I didn't have much of a choice anyway. The few miserable books lying on my shelf were all so thumbed through I had long lost any interest in them.

I immersed myself in reading but as I read I was becoming more and more aware that my eyes were running through Dante's stanzas mechanically, without taking in any meaning. I felt sleepy. It was eleven o'clock. Perfect time for a midmorning nap. And then, when the foot had burned, I'd cook myself lunch. I unclasped my watch strap and unbuckled my trouser belt. The room was cold. The fire, left unattended in favor of the kitchen stove, had died out. I wrapped myself tight in the blanket and closed my eyes. Sleep came soon after.

I woke up with a headache. My head was still full of images from my oppressive, suffocating dreams. I had dreamed a nightmare. I threw off the blanket and sat on the bed. Across the room hung a thin gray mist. And a smell of burning. I opened the window and leaned out into the frosty air of the street. My head swam. I turned back into the room and only then realized how it stank inside. Before I guessed the cause I was in the kitchen. It was dark. Thick, black smoke and that sweet, sickly stench permeated the entire room. The stove looked like a volcano. Through the gaps in the range and the hatch door spewed heavy, lazy swirls.

I retreated and shut the door. The hall too was filling with smoke. I shut myself in my room and opened the window wide. Yuk, what an awful, sticky stink ... I felt that stickiness everywhere: in my nose, on my hands, inside my mouth. I felt sick. I positioned myself by the window and, taking deep breaths, began to think through different ways of getting rid of the smoke. Alas there was only one thing to do: air the flat. A dangerous way, attracting attention but ... the only possibility. I held my breath and burst into the kitchen. I flung the window wide open and quickly ran back into my room, where the air was by now quite breathable. I wrapped myself in the blanket and covered my feet with a duvet. With my hands clasped over my chest, eyes fixed on the ceiling, I waited for the kitchen to clear. It was a method of an ostrich, perhaps, but who said I was to be constantly in a heroic mode of action? After all, so far the more energetic activity had always landed me in trouble.

But it was not granted that I should enjoy my peace for long. I heard banging on the kitchen door. A dilemma: Should I open it or not open it? Of course – open it. I could not afford the risk of having someone break down the door and poke around my flat in search of the cause of fire. Behind the door rose a clamor of female voices. Someone started pummeling the door with a fist. I called out:

"I'm coming! I'm coming ..." and turned the key.

I came face-to-face with a small group of frightened women. The poor ladies had abandoned their saucepans and hurried to my rescue. The corpulent Malinowska was holding a knife with which she was presumably cutting meat when she heard her close neighbor was in danger. Skinny, jumpy Benderowa dragged in her toddler; the look of terror in her irregular pale eyes made me want to laugh. But I stopped myself. The women swept me aside and ran in. They kept throwing questions at me, which fortunately I didn't have to answer as they were just as quickly answering them themselves, shouting over one another.

So I stood mumbling something, spreading my hands, smiling apologetically and thanking them. The women treated me with tender concern, putting into their words all their motherly affection they felt for those different twenty-year-old men – their lovers, husbands and sons – who were driving them to their graves. The energetic Piekarzowa knelt in front of the stove and began to poke about inside it with a poker. I offered my help and tried to take the poker out of her hands but was brusquely led away from the stove. It's not a job for boys. So I leaned against the sideboard and, talking to the ladies, waited for the half-burned foot to fall out of the stove. Piekarzowa put the bucket to the hatch and with a few well-practiced movements swept out a mound of ash. In a gray, acrid cloud of ash I saw the foot. It fell into the bucket. With a thud. Now Piekarzowa would look into the bucket and … I didn't want to imagine any more.

But nothing of the sort happened. The woman swept the stove clean and shut the hatch.

"Well, Mr. Jurek," she said, "it won't smoke no more. And in the future – be careful."

Nodding my head meekly, I listened to warnings and indulgent rebukes. The kitchen was emptying. The women were returning to their kitchens. Only Piekarzowa stayed for a chat, asking me about Auntie and my dead parents. At length, she commiserated over my orphaned state and Auntie's toil – "after all, an old person."

At long last I managed to get rid of the ghastly woman. I sat down in the middle of the kitchen totally crushed. In front of the stove I noticed a piece of Auntie's leg still lying there. It was incomprehensible how they could not have seen it. I poked around the bucket and found the foot, charred but still retaining its natural shape. The good housewife missed that too. No doubt I was incredibly lucky, but somehow it didn't make me jump for joy. My lunch, which I prepared all by myself – the cutlets, so keenly anticipated by my taste buds – all went down the tube. And now the flat was cold as a doghouse. My first response was to take the foot with the ash and dispose of it in the rubbish bin outside. I knew it was risky but then it was already the second day and I still hadn't got rid of one piece of my deceased.

However, I refrained from that desperate step. Resigned, I picked up the foot and the piece of leg and carried them to the bathroom where I placed them on both sides of the corpse. Then, from the sheets, I selected the biggest one and covered the corpse as neatly as I could. Only one leg and the shorter stump were sticking out from under this improvised shroud.

The time for my university lectures approached. Having checked that the flat was more or less free of smoke, I closed the windows and went out. I had my lunch in the corner bar. I chewed the bits of the overseasoned stew but they grew only bigger in my mouth. I washed them down with a beer. It was flat and sour. I quickly paid the bill and went out onto the street. I checked my watch. It turned out I was about fifteen minutes early. These fifteen minutes would have to be killed loitering and window-shopping, or reading film posters hanging outside the cinema on my way. I was not interested in the merchandise on display and I'd read the film posters several times before, but I stopped both before the shops and before the cinema. I didn't want to arrive too early.

The lecture was just like all the others I had attended so far. The cold barrenness of the walls and the ritual inventory hanging behind a framed showcase were exactly as they were before. I noted down some of the professor's words absentmindedly, though not more absentmindedly than usual. His bony, shortsighted assistant was noting the professor's every word, turning his head in a funny way like a blind sparrow hawk. After forty-five minutes the professor put his coat on and went out for a fifteen-minute break. Then he returned and got on with his lecture for another three quarters of an hour. The assistant knew well when his moment would come, and when the old man pulled out his watch he put his pen aside and waited in readiness. Then he jumped up, took the professor's coat off the coat hanger and before the old man managed even to put it on properly, he was offering him hat and walking stick. It always went like this so I was not surprised by today's ceremony.

I nipped out for a smoke. In the corridor by the window stood Alina, a girl with very bad legs, and vulgar Eva, talking in a conspiratorial way, totally absorbed in each other. A few smoking boys gathered in a small noisy group. I caught fragments of some old crass joke, which had ceased to amuse me when I was sixteen. Luckily, Mazan was not there. Instead, another student came up to me and asked if I had managed to sort out something I was supposed to arrange for the party. I replied that I had not, yet, but that I would for sure. Because I was not inclined to keep up the conversation he soon left me in peace.

Nothing had changed here. My act, punishable by the gallows, appeared pointless and unimportant. That very same lecture hall, the dark corridor and the loneliness that accompanied me so I was among these people, whom I didn't need, who couldn't help me or even harm me. After the lectures I quickly sneaked outside. Yet walking down the street I regretted my rashness. It was too early again. I couldn't think what to do with the evening. The flat was cold and I had no strength left to do any more burning. I slowed down, and then turned back toward the center. Something was nagging me about the corpse at home, and the need to get back and do something about it. I ran through in my mind a short list of friends I could visit. Somehow I didn't feel like talking to any of them. But still, I kept walking.

I remembered it was a Saturday. I was definitely too young to spend a Saturday night moping around at home. Even a home shared with a corpse. I checked several cinemas but all of them had long lines. Dejected, I stood on the curb and stared stupidly at the yellow splashes of electric light from the lampposts reflected on the street and frozen puddles. Across the street I noticed two people I knew. They were students at the Academy of Fine Arts. Nice guys. I used to go to school with one of them; we even became friends. At first I wanted to turn and walk away. But then remembered I had nowhere to walk to. I quickly crossed the street and accosted them. We greeted one another in a noisy, friendly fashion. My friends were burdened with bottles of vodka and invited me enthusiastically to help them lighten their load.

I accepted. Immediately, the mood turned light and warm. The conversation became noisy, punctuated with loud bursts of laughter. In Jacek's flat we found waiting for us two other boys and Hilda, a medical student. Hilda was wonderfully ugly, skinny as a pole and gracelessly tall. But she wore a funny little pigtail and could out-drink any boy. Without wasting time on spurious conversations we got down to it. It's hard to imagine a better place for drinking large amounts of plain vodka than Jacek's room. It was very small yet oddly bleak. It had something of a train station waiting room about it. The space between the wall and the wardrobe was crammed with rolls of canvas.

"Eat, take a bite," Jacek invited us to rolls and sausage served on grease paper.

So we ate and took bites. But most of all we drank. There were no glasses. We drank from heavy clay cups. Bottoms up. By the third round a great discussion broke out about art, politics, philosophy and ethics. We spoke all at once, with great wit and passion. One of the boys, Janek ... yes, Janek – picked up a guitar and started strumming it. We broke into a song. Soon I had drunk my fill, but the vodka had to be finished. The cups clacked again. One of the boys disappeared down the hallway and returned after a while rather pale and with wet hair. I felt I would soon follow suit. I was seeing drifting black clouds and felt a sweet acerbic taste in my mouth. Now people regularly disappeared behind the door, returned and drank on. Only Hilda didn't move, sitting ramrod straight throughout, though she drank the most.

We reached the point of soul-searching and confessions. Jacek put his arm around me and poured out his heart. He swore his undying friendship, pledged his life to creating great art and threatened to show someone what's what. Before long we were embracing and kissing as true friends. In the process we knocked the table and one of the cups fell on the floor. Next I was in someone else's arms. Again we hugged and opened our hearts. I had had about enough. I was burning with the fire of impatience. I got up and, swaying, headed for the coatrack.

"Jurek, where are you going?" someone grabbed my arm.

"I'm going," I mumbled. "I must ..."

Now more hands grabbed me and threw me on the bed. Everyone talked at me. A new cup of vodka was put under my nose. I leaped to my feet and turned over the table.

"Fools!" I screamed, "I have a corpse at home! I'm a murderer! A murderer!..."

With outstretched arms I tried to reach the door. Somewhere on the way I tripped over a stool and crashed to the floor. My head was booming just like a bathtub struck with an axe.

"I'm a murderer, ha ha ha ..." I cried, picking myself up off the floor.

"What are you doing?!" shouted Jacek. "Be quiet ...! Peasant ..."

"Leave him alone," said Hilda soberly. "He's completely drunk."

5

WALKING DOWN THE STREET, I SAW DOUBLE. I DON'T THINK
I had ever experienced that before. I amused myself by
guessing which of the twin objects was real. And usually I got it right. Yet my trousers were wet from wading
through imaginary puddles. I vomited lightly and without
any difficulties. I was balancing on the pavement, courteously giving passersby a wide berth. I was trying to sing
out loud, but my throat was dry and my voice came out
raspy. I came to a little square with two lonely benches. I
dragged myself to one of them and keeled over. Immediately everything around me began to sway. The instabil-
ity of my position instantly released the dynamic volatil-
ity of the world. So I changed my position. I stretched
out on the bench with my head hanging down and legs
thrown over the back. The world viewed from this van-
tage point, through the prism of alcohol, seemed for the
first few seconds quite interesting. But it didn't last long.
I had to change my position again, as this one wasn't very
comfortable. Carefully handling the absurd weight of my
head, I arranged my body into ever-different configura-
tions. Now I sat on the armrest with raised arms. Then I
changed into an ape, then into a hero. I blessed the alcohol that allowed me to assume all those forms. Eventually,
I let go of the bench and moved on. I stopped for a moment and raised my finger:

"No one will learn about the corpse," I whispered
conspiratorially.

The pavement on the street where I stood was glisten-
ing and looked slippery. I hesitated before stepping onto

it like before stepping into a river. Suddenly I heard the drum of horses' hooves. In the perspective of the street loomed an ornamented coach pulled by two horses. I recognized a hearse. The horses ran at a trot and the hearse was quickly approaching. Enthralled and elated, I opened out my arms.

"Oh, you drivers of death!" I greeted them, "I envy you. And admire you. Oh how I admire you. How lightly, blithely and gracefully you carry off death! While I ... I'm tired of it, I – a miserable murderer. Ah, why do I bother ... I rejoice in your triumph. And thou, Cerberus with a peasant face ... thou, that's right – thou!..."

The hearse was almost level with me now and as I spat out the "thou" I pointed my finger at the face of the coachman dressed in funereal garb:

"Ha ha ha!... Ride on, my hero. I shall farm my little bloody field myself. With the saw! With the axe! I kill ... I kill ..."

The hearse was vanishing in a whirr of turning wheels and trotting hooves. I followed it with my eyes and said in a hollow voice:

"As old Goethe used to say, as old Goethe used to say ..."

I moved on with my open arms. I felt strong and free. The annihilation of the corpse seemed an easy task again. The sense of power exhilarated me.

"I'm free through murder!" I cried out. "Freeeeee!..."

As soon as the words died on my lips I was arrested. I didn't even try to resist. Two policemen held me fast in a way that precluded any attempt at breaking loose. I let them lead me away in peace and humility. I was trying to carry myself with dignity. Not to tremble, or rattle my teeth. I thought bitterly that my freedom hadn't lasted long. Not even forty-eight hours from the terrible deed. How long is forty-eight hours? There are twelve hours to the daytime. Twelve and twelve.

I was intrigued by the forthcoming trial and the prospect of being hanged. I didn't feel bad at all except for the paralyzing fear of being beaten. I resolved to tell everything as soon as we arrived somewhere. I considered my chances of getting away with it. Very slim. Almost the entire corpse lay in my bath. Ah, but it probably lies there no more. They must have taken it away for forensics. But then they may have left it there under guard – hm, I wonder what he looks like, this man sitting in my flat now – and are going to lead me there. God, I hope they don't beat me. I could hardly control the trembling.

The vodka evaporated now. There was only fear. I saw the neon letters on the police station. The booking room made a ghastly and somber impression on me. The only light was a desk lamp, which had no lamp shade and cast huge shadows of people and objects on the walls. I took in the drab furnishings: the desk behind a barrier, two chairs, a scratched bench. It crossed my mind that in a few minutes I might be laying on that bench, naked, bleeding and trembling. Proudly I raised my head. Standing so, with my face like a mask, I tried to think of the scornful grimace I should adopt for the first question.

They pushed me toward the barrier. I looked straight in the face of the on-duty sergeant behind the desk. It didn't make any impression on him. They took away my wallet, my belt and my shoelaces. Luckily my trousers hung well without the belt and I could still look a hero. The policemen weren't showing any interest in my person, which hurt my feelings. They just chatted among themselves, sluggishly. I couldn't follow their conversation, as the vodka began to swoosh in my head again. One of the policemen, a weakling, shorter than me, to which I took personal offense, escorted me down a dark corridor to a heavy, steel-clad door. The bolt clanged and I was pushed inside a cold, unlit cell.

I stood rooted to my spot. I didn't dare to make a move. I couldn't see a thing. From the corners of the cell came animal-like grunts. Slowly my eyes grew used to the darkness. I began to get a sense of the dwarfish proportions of the cell. But I decided not to leave my spot. Suddenly I felt a live force grab me by the feet. Some enormous boa constrictor began winding itself around my legs. Roaring and choking, I grasped at the wall. The pressure eased momentarily, only to squeeze itself tighter. A large, heavy body was performing some terrifying convolutions around my feet. I stood patient as a sea rock. Based on the alternating rhythm of pounding and panting I came to the conclusion that there were in fact two bodies. But I was not sure. The hand which leaned against the wall and with which I was supporting myself was beginning to throb from the effort. At long last the bodies let go of my feet and crawled away into the deeps of the den.

With my back against the wall I slowly shuffled into a corner, where I sat down. The worn-out drunks were now lying in a writhing heap in the opposite corner. I thought that for my crime I was to suffer not only through the interrogation and execution but also a Golgotha of humiliation. Reducing me to the level of these drunks seemed to me particularly cruel. Their primitive noises kindled in me the fire of hatred. Meanwhile, having rested a bit, the pair resumed their orgiastic antics. I could now distinguish the movements of this creepy octopus. It wasn't howling now but purred in a monotonous, almost plaintive fashion, locked on the clay floor in a weird dance, accompanied by a hollow thumping. Suddenly the corridor echoed with steps. The drunks grew still. Through my body ran a funny shudder, all the way from my toes to the top end of my spine. I felt a touch of chill on my cheeks. I rearranged my legs in readiness to spring to my feet but waited with dignity. When the door opened I was ready. I didn't want to get up without an order.

The order didn't come. Instead a small, inconspicuous-looking man was pushed through the door, and the bolt clanged shut. There was nothing left to do but to kill time by observing the new arrival. The little man was sober. He looked around the cell without inhibition and said in a half voice:

"Blessed be the Lord."

"*In saecula saeculorum*, amen," I replied politely.

The drunks, feeling secure again, resumed their mumbling and writhing on the floor.

"May I take a pew with you?" asked the little man without moving from his spot.

"But of course," I agreed.

He approached with a mincing step and sat down next to me. In the faint light from the street I could make out a rough outline of his features. The little man was probably coming to the end of his mature years. He had a small but fine figure, and a beautiful profile. Ah, how many Romans had I seen in the corner bar where I ate my dinner. He didn't have a coat. His modest, threadbare attire hung on him faultlessly. He was, perhaps, the last earthly companion to treat me in a kindly, human fashion. So I looked at him closely. The little man was sitting still but I felt emanating from him manly energy and concentration. After a few minutes he turned to me:

"Do you think they will be able to understand my reasons?"

"I don't think they are capable of understanding anyone's reasons," I said. "Neither yours nor mine."

"You are right," he agreed. "I will be taken for a relic thief."

"Undoubtedly."

"Funny, that," smiled the relic thief. "The consistent following of God's commandments always leads man astray ... Were you surprised by my greeting everyone here?"

"No."

"Excellent. I have nothing to say to people who are

surprised by simple words. Such people bore me terribly. But it seems to me that you, sir, despite your tender age, have already acquired the wisdom of not being surprised by simple things."

"Why do they take you for a relic thief?" I asked.

"Ah, this ..." he smiled. " I stole a golden arm."

"From the Capuchin church? I know this golden arm well."

"From the tone of your voice, sir, I conclude that you have lived in the New Town for a time and are familiar with the magic of the golden arm. I was troubled by it too, and more painfully than you, and for much longer. I'm twice your age. I'm forty-seven years old, nearly fifty."

"The golden arm was, if I'm correct, given to the abbey in the seventeenth century."

"Sixteenth. Your error is actually perfectly excusable, for it happened at the beginning of the Baroque period. In 1598 to be precise. Kazimierz Hermanowicz joined the order and the arm was kept in the abbey's treasury. Only after his death in 1610 was it put on public display, thus fixing the conviction that the arm was in fact given to the order in the seventeenth century."

"Do you know other details connected with Hermanowicz?"

"Oh yes. The question of the golden arm has interested me for a long time. The moment I heard God's voice telling me to steal it, I began to study the matter in earnest."

"Did you hear God's voice?"

"Huh, let's not simplify this ..."

I didn't hear the rest of the relic thief's answer. The drunks, after a rest, burst out with their madness again. One of them snatched the other's belt with his teeth and now both were chewing on it, growling and tugging at it, each to himself. This tug of war went on for a while until an apocalyptic roar communicated to us that one of the drunks had lost his tooth. The thrashing on the floor stopped. Out came sobbing and words of succor. At last the two bodies rose and began to urinate in silence against the opposite wall.

"You were asking," resumed my interlocutor, "if I heard the voice of God. I think we should not pose the question this way. I am not one for spewing revelations. God's will speaks to us without any metaphysical packaging. It simply manifests itself through certain decisions and thoughts in our brain. Through a certain order of events in our lives. I, my dear sir, have been dealing in sacrilegious thieving for a long time now. But they were mostly trifles."

"Trifles?"

"Yes. Do you remember that little cherub with a porcelain head, nodding thanks every time someone put a coin in the box? He was my benefactor for two years. Every week I knelt before the box, sunk in prayer, during which I would pick the lock with a needle and take out the coins. I was caught by accident, in a silly way, as usual. Later I was involved in other sacrilegious thefts. Small votive candles, and once I had a go at a chalice. But a serious matter like the golden arm I hadn't tried before. It's a difficult case. It's possible I will rot for the rest of my life in jail."

"Couldn't you try a psychiatrist?" I was worried I may have offended the sacrilegious thief but he showed no sign of taking offense.

"It's my only hope," he replied gently, "but whether it's going to be successful this time remains to be seen. It's already helped me once, when I was put on trial for the chalice. I shammed it rather badly and they didn't believe me. Only when I started explaining the true philosophical motivation behind my actions did the doctor write out a certificate that saved me from five years in prison. I think now I have to take a similar route. Tell the truth.

Truth opens the gates of heaven. It's interesting how many people claim to be following the teachings of Christ yet practically no one understands their true sense. So far it's served me well. They take me for a madman. And yet it's so childishly simple, like the sunshine. Since God created the sacred, he had to create the sacrilegious. Since at the root of our religion lies the legend about a murder, it's natural that murderers have to exist. You killed a man ..."

I shuddered. The sacrilegious thief didn't notice and continued:

"In your case, the primitive desire of enriching oneself or exacting revenge ..."

"I didn't kill to enrich myself, or out of revenge," I interrupted him.

"Oh, I'm sorry, I didn't mean to pry into your personal affairs," the sacrilegious thief apologized politely.

I said in an unnaturally high voice:

"I simply killed."

"That's OK too, young man," my companion smiled gently, and then asked:

"Are you a believer? Please excuse the forthrightness of my question."

"No."

"I thought so. The youth of today is mostly unbelieving. Without unbelievers the church would not exist. But I do hope one day you will find your path to God."

"It's very kind of you to wish me well," I replied politely. "Trouble is, I have very little time left to find that path ..."

"Hm, true," smiled the sacrilegious thief. "But let us be of good faith."

My conversation with this kind man absorbed me to such an extent that I didn't hear the steps in the corridor. When, pulled roughly by my sleeve, I was leaving the cell, my companion didn't even send me a parting look. In the other corner the two drunks were snoring away, soaked in urine and blood.

"Student ... Yes ... Very well ... Which college?"

I gave the name of my university. The desk sergeant looked at me sternly and disapprovingly. The policeman standing next to him smiled.

"A learned man," he opined spitefully.

I was very ashamed. I stood humbly in my socks, holding up my falling trousers. They still had my shoes and belt. There came a moment of weighty, contemptuous silence. I smiled differentially.

"Citizen Officer," I said, "Saturday. It happens ..." and opened my arms in a gesture of hopelessness.

The duty officer liked it. He didn't smile, but in his eyes there flickered a brief, humorous spark. He frowned and asked:

"How much did you shell out yesterday?"

"I wasn't paying."

"Hm ..." The duty officer began to leaf through the papers and engaged in a conversation with the policeman. It went on for ages.

I used every moment they turned their heads to arrange my face into a sneering grimace. Apart from the three of us there was also a young lady in a scarlet fur. She had come to the station to ask about her fiancé, a petty thief with whom she had spent the night. The woman was richly rouged, pretty and full of scorn. Her presence embarrassed me greatly. I felt deep shame in her presence, what with my dishevelment and the whole jail situation. She wasn't looking at me at all, which hurt even more. At long last the duty officer finished his conversation, rose from his chair, put his hands in his pockets and began pacing the room. He stopped at the window and looked through the windowpanes with calm concentration. Then he came up to the locker and took out my student card, my belt and the shoes.

"Get dressed," he said. "I hope I won't see you here again."

I wished that more fervently than he could ever guess.

6

THE RELIEF WHICH FILLED ME TO THE BRIM AFTER LEAVING the police station, at home turned into depression. Sitting on the bed I ruminated on my merciless fate, which kept throwing me higgledy-piggledy into cruel, humiliating adventures. The thought that I had just brushed against the gallows, in fact slipped through the noose, didn't give me any satisfaction. I had made a fool of myself. Cringing and cursing myself, I recalled the details of the past night. The memory of my drunken exploits at Jacek's pressed so heavily on my mind that even though I was already lying in a half-slumber, I extricated myself from the bedsheets and snatched my coat.

With pitiless stubbornness I played back the infamous episodes, my childishness, my stupidity and my fall. And then, suddenly, came the fear. I knew fear well. It had come to me several times in the last few days, with greater or lesser force. The new attack was dangerous. I recalled with terrifying clarity how I'd screamed at Jacek's, "I'm a murderer!," how I drank, how I kept saying in the street, "Now I'll cut her head off!" moments before being stopped by the police.

It was six in the morning. The hangman's hour. Shaking with cold and terror I lay fully dressed on the bed and pulled the sheets over my head. But the calm wasn't coming. I leaped out of bed and with all my strength started slapping my face. In spite of my faint, frozen body I threw off my jacket, sweater and shirt, and began to exercise vigorously. I tortured myself with sit-ups, push-ups and handstands, listening to my pounding heart and wheezing breath. I ran to the bathroom and put my head under the tap, then began massaging myself with karate chops and kneading my muscles until I was in pain. Then I got dressed and went back to the kitchen. I put the kettle on the stove and made myself a cup of hot tea.

Gritting my teeth and determined, I returned to the bathroom. The saw and the axe were already there. The fear had left me, as always when I focused on a concrete job. I pulled the sheet off the corpse. Rolled my sleeves up. And began to saw the other leg. I used the tried-and-tested method. First the foot, then the calf.

Shrrt-shrrt ... shrrt-shrrt ... shrrt-shrrt ...

When I'd shortened the second leg just like the first one, I had a break. I allowed myself a cigarette. It was tasteless. I went back to work. With a few short blows of the axe I crushed both knees. I turned the top of the toilet seat into a workbench where I laid out the axe, saw and an open penknife. Taking turns with these tools I managed to disconnect the stumps from the rest of the body. Now the corpse lay comfortably in the bath. It occurred to me that I had made a terrible mistake in not bleeding the corpse while it was still warm. I would have had a much easier job. But it was too late for regrets. With the penknife I cut through the dress on the torso and peeled it off bit by bit. Without disturbing the corpse I managed to bare it completely. I rolled the rags into a ball and stuffed it behind the kitchen stove.

That was all I could do with the corpse in this position. To proceed with severing the remaining limbs the corpse had to be repositioned. I thought about it for a while, then grabbed it under the arms and lifted it. The effort was killing me. Soon I felt hammers banging on my temples. The corpse began to put up resistance again. The lolling head just would not rest on the rim of the bath. I wasn't giving up, though. With all my muscles strained to the limit, I pulled the corpse up over the bathtub's edge.

I gave it another pull and when the resting point came to about halfway down the back, it finally kept its balance. I began to saw. I was trying to steer the saw away from the ribs so it cut only through the flesh. When I reached the spine my arms were numb and black wispy blotches floated before my eyes. But I didn't want to stop the work halfway through. I sawed on. The body began to quiver and tilt. I mobilized all my energies to keep it steady. At last the spine gave in. From then on it was all a breeze. I pushed the cut-up remains back into the bath.

The corpse ceased to be a whole. It lost its corporeal identity. Inside the bath lay the stomach and thighs, flanked by the breastbone on the one end and knees on the other; on the tile floor – an oddly proportioned bust with two large breasts, a head and very long arms. I picked it up by the hands and threw this ... shape into the bath. Then I covered the flesh with a sheet. For it was flesh. Just flesh, not a corpse. Not even a carcass. My victory over the corpse was therefore a victory only over form. The body was still in the bath and not a tiniest piece of it had been annihilated. It was, if anything, a moral victory. More like capturing of the enemy flag. The corpse had lost its flag.

The third day of my battle with the corpse was coming to an end. It should start decomposing now. In some warehouse I bought several pounds of crushed ice and laid it over the remains. Over the bathtub, I put down three small planks and placed a few of Auntie's plants on them. In the center, Auntie's collection of cacti, on the sides, a tiny papyrus and an araucaria. The bathroom acquired a very pleasant ambience. Something like a tranquil little chapel.

The following day I took one of the remains out from under the sheet. At first I couldn't work out which part of the body it was. That pleased me. I wrapped it carefully in paper and tied it with a string. On the parcel I wrote an address. I had been thinking about this address for hours, rejecting the more eccentric ideas so as not to make it look too suspicious but trying to avoid banality or unwarranted carelessness. I opted for a surname ending in the rather normal "-ski," but with a combination of preceding letters that was unusual and beautifully sonorous. I added some class to the popular name of Edward too by spelling it with a *v*. And gave the sender the witty and laconic name of Antoni Nul.

The clerk at the post office cast a critical eye over my parcel.

"What's in it?" he asked.

"Perishables," I explained.

"Write that down. Besides, it's not tied properly. There … see?" he shook the parcel and the strings began to loosen up and slip off.

I struggled contritely with the string for a long time, then timidly asked for a bit of sealing wax, with which, in all that confusion, I burned my fingers. At last the parcel was accepted.

After my lectures I bought a larger amount of string, cardboard boxes and paper. I prepared two types of ink, a pen and a pencil. I spread out a plan of the town and a map on the table. I scoured the plan in search of streets with amusing or lyrical names and wrote them down. To my fictional addressees I gave names of characters from my favorite books. I had to give those names Polish forms, which was a lot of fun. I wrote alternately with the pen and the pencil, and changed the ink. From time to time I also changed the style of writing, now making it look like the clumsy scrawls of an illiterate, at other times drawing straight lines in pencil. I remembered that among Auntie's few books was a manual of calligraphy. The old, little book, after years of neglect, was to be useful again. I studiously practiced the old-fashioned flourishes, ruining three sheets of paper in the process, until I achieved a perfect example of the old style. As the hours passed I grew calmer and hopeful. After filling those fifteen boxes and sending them out, I would proclaim victory.

At long last all the addresses were ready. I brought a piece of the body from the bathroom and started wrapping it up. Suddenly I stopped. I was overcome by a wave of fatigue. And with it – fear. I was familiar with this condition. Whenever I got absorbed in some light task – heavy manual labor was out of the question – after some time I began to feel a rising anxiety. It was a vague sense of terror, dejection and depression, which had only been temporarily tricked by my activity. Today, the anxiety was more tangible and easier to overcome. If before I was simply unable to find a logical explanation of why I was engaged in reading a particular book or puzzling out a certain test, now finding a justification for my action was straightforward and irresistible. The battle with the corpse had liberated me from those unmanly histrionics and feebleness. It was the first difficult and dangerous task I had ever faced. Although the panic attacks still happened, they had a real cause. I learned to overcome them through cold rationalization of my current situation, from which followed the choice of appropriate actions. This time, though, the fear seemed to be better grounded than usual. For as soon as someone would unpack my parcel in some remote little town, another person somewhere else would pin a little flag on the dot denoting our town on his map. The more parcels bearing stamps of my local post office that were opened in various corners of the country, the more leads for our policemen to conclude that the murder took place here rather than anywhere else. At the same time, I was aware that the day I should inform the authorities of Auntie's disappearance was getting inexorably near. The date I'd give them would have to coincide with the time of death, which would be established by forensic analysis of the remains. And that would be suspicious, for sure.

It was possible – I reasoned with myself – that my thinking was full of holes due to my lack of experience. Nevertheless it was undeniable that by sending the remains by post I was giving the detectives a certain advantage. I was disappointed. All that nice, calming work would be a waste of time. There was nothing to do but to tear up all the fictitious addresses, the inventing of which had been such a pleasant distraction; pleasant not only because it was fun but also because I believed it to be useful. Once again it crossed my mind that the annihilation of the corpse was harder than might be generally believed, that the struggle was tough and the adversary brave. So – what to do? I thought of the river. I had already been to check it out. The banks were frozen, so a parcel would have to be thrown in away from the ice. But I wouldn't dare to drop it from the bridge, even in the middle of the night. Unless I packed it all away in a sack ... A sack, I needed to buy a sack. Come on – I was getting annoyed with myself – where does one buy a sack? I went in my mind through all the shops I knew, yet I could not remember a single one where they might be selling sacks. I gave up. I was sure I'd find one. But then, who needs a sack? I'd take a few parcels and throw them into the river outside of town. I decided to go there the next day. Confidently, I wrapped the piece lying on the table and put it in the box. Then started slowly tearing up the labels with fictitious addresses.

Still, the moment I tore up the first paper, the doubts returned. I took the parcel out to the bathroom and stretched myself out on the bed. My experience with the corpse had taught me to avoid harried, unpremeditated actions. I thought that by giving the authorities the advantage in sending the parcels by post I could immediately turn this advantage ... to my advantage. OK, tomorrow morning, at an anonymous post office, my parcel would arrive bearing the postmark of our town. But what if another post office receives a parcel bearing a postmark of another town? And the day after tomorrow another parcel with another piece of the corpse would be stamped in another town altogether? Even if they eventually came to the conclusion that there's one murderer, how would they decide his true address? Rather, they would assume that mailing the parcels from different towns was a deliberate ploy. How could they tell that the murderer would start with his hometown? Such a perfidious criminal would know to steer clear of any post office near his permanent address. Who knows, maybe it would be a dot without a flag that would come to be the focus of the investigation? I went on honing my plan. I rejected the idea of visiting several towns in a row. That would be too expensive. Moreover, what excuse would I give at the university for absenting myself from the lectures? Still, the advantage, once relinquished to the enemy, had to be immediately turned around. Tomorrow I would take three parcels and mail them from the main post office in a big town two hours away by train. That should be a big enough stick in the spokes of the investigation. The rest of the body I would dispose of here by different methods.

From the pile of addresses on the table I picked out those that struck me as the funniest and returned to the packing. The overall weight of the parcels was one hundred and twenty pounds. I took them out to the bathroom and burned the papers with addresses.

7

Traveling had always held a certain attraction for me. In my modest experience I had traveled little and every trip, even the shortest one, was for me a source of amusement and an adventure. In a different town I felt a bit like a foreigner. It was still before midday when I had all the parcels posted and so I went for a stroll around the town. Luckily, it was warm and sunny. Mailing the parcels was a big step forward. Pleased with the progress, I decided to spend the rest of my time in town on small pleasures. When I got tired walking the streets I stepped into a café. I treated myself to a big coffee and two cakes. I had my lunch in a good restaurant, choosing the menu with the sedulous care of a gourmet. After lunch I felt a little tired. My return train was in the evening. Wandering around, I came across a cinema. They were showing a movie it was impossible to get tickets for in my town, but here I bought one without trouble.

Movies make me feel vulnerable and leaving a cinema is almost always a nasty shock. The exotic glamour of the strange town was shattered, showing all its fragility. The station was merely dirty and noisy. Many times I have promised myself to go to the cinema every day, to spend much of my time – I was afraid to say: life – in lethargy. I never fulfilled my promise.

The compartment was not overcrowded. Opposite me sat a girl, reading a book. She was pretty. I was observing her with pleasure, the light auburn lock of hair on her forehead, a small nose, her dark, resolute eyebrows. She had delicate, shapely hands. With sadness I thought that soon she would leave the compartment and I'd stay behind, alone with sleeping workers, or maybe she'd get off the train with me in our town, but then we'd lose each other in the crowd. I would be left alone. Almost with gratitude I thought about my corpse, the struggle with whom somehow filled my loneliness.

The train was moving at a sleepy pace. We were passing the scattered lights of villages and small towns. The lightbulb hanging from the ceiling gave faint, murky light. How can she read? – I thought about the girl. And without any premeditated plan, I said:

"You will damage your eyes."

The girl quickly raised her head and frowned lightly. Then she smiled and put away her book.

"Thank you," she smiled again. "I'm used to it, they always tell me off for reading in the dark."

"And quite rightly too," I replied solemnly.

We started to chat. At first I was afraid that our light, casual conversation would suddenly break off after some trivial remark, that after a few stops, before we reached our town we would fall silent, running out of things to say. But as we spoke the risk of that happening faded away. We slowly relaxed into our chat and the moments of silence that fell from time to time between sentences did not separate us. We were silent together. At some point I felt the girl's hand on my knee. I appreciated the gesture but still didn't dare touch her hand.

We were smoking cigarettes in the empty corridor. In a distance, far from the tracks, passed the lights of some settlement.

"When I was little," said the girl, "I believed that those lights were elves' lanterns. During the day the elves slept and no one knew about them. But at night they would come out onto the hills and light their lights. The oldest elf, their king, lit a red lantern. Me and my brother were always looking for the red lantern of the king. Did you believe in elves?"

"Of course."

"Your answer lacks conviction. I sense the irredeemable influence of a rationalistic upbringing."

"But you are still very young."

"Ah, you old men ... I see you have acquired the arcane art of old-fashioned gallantry ... Never mind, let's look for the red elf."

"So far we haven't been very successful."

"So what. The greater the effort, the sweeter the reward. O look, there ... the green one. He is also an important elf. Though he is far below the red king."

"I understand that the kingdom of elves has its own bureaucratic hierarchy. I wonder who is in charge of the elven field workers?"

"Boring realist. It's clear you never believed in elves."

"I assure you, I did, but ..."

"But?"

"But I stopped. I simply grew up and started thinking seriously about the future."

"Very commendable."

"Very. And by the way, I'd gladly give a big part of my life – I don't have any other capital – to someone who could convince me there is a future."

"Hm, a Hamlet too."

"Yes. A Hamlet. But unlike thousands of other native Hamlets, I have at my disposal a real skull."

"Strongly put."

"I'm sorry, I won't bore you any more." Suddenly my spirits flagged.

"Hey, what's wrong ...?"

"Nothing. Nothing worth talking about."

"But why? We can talk. It's high time ..."

I smiled bashfully.

"I'm very pleased we met. I hope we'll meet again."

"Well, I'll live in hope."

ANDRZEJ BURSA

We stood in silence. I was focused, filled with blossoming joy.

"It's really great ..." I mumbled after a while.

"What?"

"That I've found the red elf!" I cried out, pointing quickly at a red light glowing in the distance.

We both burst out laughing.

8

It was a clear, starry night. I was returning from my date with Teresa. I walked with my head high, listening with pleasure to the sound of my steps echoing off the pavement. "Teresa, Teresa," sang my youth. Barely four days had passed from our first meeting and I was already riding the high crest of my love. With the submissiveness of a weak character – which I'd been told I had – I allowed Teresa to take over all my thoughts and imagination. Even when I was thinking about other things somewhere through the back of my mind's eye passed the images of her face, her smile, her eyelashes with snowflakes on them or her hands in old leather gloves, which had became a holy relic to me.

We saw each other every day. We both had no doubt it was love. "Love, love," I kept saying to myself aloud when alone in my flat. I hadn't neglected the corpse. Fortunately the cold weather held fast so the regularly replenished ice kept the body from decomposing. Only once during the last three days had I wrapped some innards up in paper and discarded them on the suburban rubbish dump often visited by ravens and cats. That trip cost me a lot of time and effort and the result was rather measly. Once more I had to admit that the corpse was a tough opponent and fighting it required a lot of willpower, courage and ingenuity. I hadn't given it much time lately but I wanted to bring it to an end as soon as possible. I was getting bored with it.

I was slowly coming to the conclusion that the period when the struggle with the corpse filled the void in my life was over. The corpse had been replaced by Teresa. Yet I could not accept this conclusion without reservations. I knew that a woman could not fulfill or replace all the various longings and desires that tore at my soul; I knew that nurturing my love for Teresa would mean killing it, too. And yet, under the influence of this girl I was beginning to recover my faith in life. I knew it was an illusion, and I kept telling myself so. I had wasted too many years dreaming about traveling, adventures and the exciting life that awaited me. (Too many times I had been punished for my dreams by everyday objects in our flat, by the lecture hall, by all that machinery of terror that closed up on me, seemingly forever.) Yet when I was with Teresa I felt calm and believed, against all reason, that I was still destined for great things.

These fanciful musings seemed to be confirmed by my recent experiences. After all, killing Auntie and struggling with the corpse was definitely something. And my situation as a man standing between the gallows and an unknown adventure was not devoid of a certain dramatic grandeur. Nevertheless, it's not exactly the kind of drama I had in mind, not the sort of deed that Teresa's knight should be famous for. Such and similar thoughts crossed my mind in those days. Those thoughts and reflections were rather superfluous, unable to affect the great lightness that filled me. The pangs of fear still happened. I was aware that I was pushing my luck, dragging my feet about reporting to the police while doing nothing about getting rid of the remains.

In such moments my head would explode with brilliant ideas of annihilating the corpse. Once, as I was falling asleep with the image of Teresa under my eyelids, I was gripped by a spasm of fear. Any attempt to talk myself out of it and stay in bed were in vain. I dragged myself out from between the sheets and went into the kitchen. I rummaged through the sideboard and found the meat grinder.

With some difficulty I clamped it to the edge of the table, picked out a few chunks of dead meat and began to mince. My plan was terrifyingly simple, with the simple ingenuity of a perpetuum mobile. I would mix the minced meat with the ash from the stove in the bucket and then take it out as usual in the morning and dump it in the rubbish bin. As I earnestly turned the crank the work brought me peace, as it usually did. I thought of Teresa. Of our walks in the spring, which was just round the corner. Of alleys lined with young birch trees, of orchards, of those little white-and-yellow flowers which blossomed on the shrubs in spring. I was smiling and muttering to myself. Suddenly my bliss was shuttered by an excruciating pain. I had caught my finger in the meat grinder. I yanked my hand out and put it to my mouth, but dropped it immediately as the odor of the meat hit my nostrils. I picked up the crank again but without the previous enthusiasm. The work slowed. The grinder was getting jammed. I gave up. I was a picture of pathetic horror: standing in my pajamas working a bloody meat grinder in the cold kitchen in the middle of the night. Now my brilliant idea seemed idiotic. My mind drifted over to the question of how to disinfect the grinder. I threw the minced meat in the bucket and after some hesitation, the other two pieces, as well; after I stirred it all up, the ash covered the pieces so thoroughly they could not raise any suspicions. I went back to bed. The moment I closed my eyes the image of Teresa appeared before me to guide me into sleep.

I managed to get home just before the gates were locked. I was pleased I didn't have to struggle with the massive rusty key. I ran up the steps and saw before my door two small human figures. Light shock gave place to amused annoyance. I recognized my granny and her daughter, Auntie's sister. They both lived in a small town in the mountains, a good dozen miles away from the railway station. Auntie, and what she sent them, was their only livelihood. Granny, who was pushing eighty, suffered from chronic eye pain and smeared them with an iridescent white paste. It made her look like a strange bird. Seeing her, I always thought that if the biblical term "whitewashed tomb" actually existed, she would be it. Her daughter, a fifty-year-old virgin, was handicapped and wore very thick glasses, without which she was practically blind. Apart from that she suffered from a serious stomach disorder, and played the violin. I remember a visit we paid them a few years ago in their hometown. It was a warm September evening. A golden stream of sunshine flowed through an open window. It was a golden, lyrical moment. Aunt Emilia stood by the window, hidden from the courtyard behind the curtain, and played. I can't remember the melody except that it was old and sad. When we entered the room she stopped and blushed like a schoolgirl. We had to plead with her for a long time to play something again. At long last, blushing and excusing herself, she agreed to repeat the concert. I remember vividly Granny's face beaming with almost lewd pleasure as she listened to the tones of violin, and Auntie's – approving but unemotional. I remember that I hated her then. Who knows, maybe here I'd be able to find the roots of my deed, if I could be bothered.

I sat the old ladies down and began to set the table. They both protested that they would not eat, even though they were hungry and watched my every move heralding the imminent appearance of food with growing excitement. It amused me. I put the kettle on and made a pile of sandwiches. I used up all the cheese, which was supposed to last me three days. I worked quickly and with confidence. A week of self-reliance had taught me a lot. I told the women that Auntie had left for a long business trip and tried to assuage their worries about the lack of letters and a money order. When supper was finally on the table, the women rose to say a prayer. I got up too. Until now on these occasions I always stood with my hands casually clasped behind my back and a blasé expression on my face. But the experience of the last few days cured me of my adolescent arrogance. I bowed my head lightly and clasped my hands in front of me. Toward the end I even made a vague gesture with my right hand. We sat down. The old girls ate with appetite. I excused myself and peeked into the bathroom. The corpse was well covered. When the ladies began to yawn I made a bed for them in the room, and for myself laid a mattress on the kitchen floor. It was hard and uncomfortable.

"Oyey! ... Yey, yey!..." I heard Aunt Emilia screaming in the bathroom.

I jumped up and switched the light on. Groping my way through the hallway, I ran to see what happened. Aunt Emilia in her long nightdress was sitting in the bath with her feet high above her head. She was holding a lit candle in one hand while the other hand was making desperate waving movements.

"Who's here?" she stammered when I appeared in the doorway.

"It's me, Auntie," I said as calmly as I could. "What happened?"

Aunt Emilia started gibbering again.

"There is someone lying here ..."

I got scared. Aunt Emilia had discovered the corpse. She had to be killed. If I did it now, while she was still in the bath, I would spare myself the trouble of transporting her corpse. But then I'd have to kill Granny too. Three corpses on one head. No, that would be too much. I took Aunt Emilia's hand and pulled her out of the bath.

"Someone's lying there," she was shaking with horror. "Jurek, dear, who's there?"

Trying to calm her, I carefully examined the bath. The depression indicated the place where the stomach and the lower part of the body lay. I knew the arrangement of my corpse very well and could determine precisely the position of each body part under the sheet. Aunt Emilia had landed on the best-preserved part when she fell in. She had mistaken the bath for the loo. She was still very upset.

"Someone is lying there ... I think ... I felt it ..." she kept repeating.

I took the candle out of her hand and bent over the bath.

"But Auntie," I explained calmly, "it's only linen. Look, there ..." I carefully unfolded the sheet. I manipulated the candle in such a way so she could not see anything. Emilia was straining her sick eyes. She was calming down. Suddenly, when it seemed the danger was over, the light came on.

"Damn," I cried out and raised my hand to my eyes as if blinded by the light. At the same time I pushed my elbow into her face, knocking off her glasses. "Oh, I'm so sorry!"

The bathroom was flooded with light now. Aunt Emilia stood by numbly, rubbing her face. She couldn't see a thing. I took her gently by the arm and led her away to her bed. On our way we met Granny, who was awakened by the noise in the bathroom. She was wearing a white turban.

I fell into a heavy uncomfortable sleep, from which I soon awoke. Only now it struck me how much I'd grown used to sharing my loneliness with the corpse. The nocturnal presence of two old women in the house irritated and distracted me. I couldn't go back to sleep. In the surrounding silence I picked out the slightest noise, barely audible squeaks of the furniture, the hollow, intermittent song of the kitchen tap. As my ears tuned in to those susurrations I could clearly distinguish the breathing of two sleeping women despite being separated from them by two closed doors and a hallway. Then the breathing stopped and changed into whispers. I couldn't hear the words but the conversation grew louder, the beds squeaked and the room filled with a gentle bustle.

After a few moments I heard the clanking of plates and cutlery. At first weak and timid, the clanking soon intensified until it sounded as if a noisy feast was under way in my room. Only the dinner conversation was missing. There were still some leftovers from supper on the table in the dining room and the old girls were apparently clearing them off. When the bustle died out I heard the women tiptoeing toward the kitchen. As carefully as I could I rearranged myself on the mattress. I wanted to be able to observe them without arousing their suspicion. The women slipped into the kitchen and slowly approached my bed. Granny stretched out her hand and scratched me lightly on my nose, I didn't move. Then she whispered:

"He's sleeping, good boy ..."

"God bless him ..." said Aunt Emily.

Assured, they turned away. The older led the younger, who in the dark probably couldn't see anything. They were heading for the sideboard but bumped into the low, broad kitchen table on which I had left a bit of bread and sausage. They bent over the table and searched it thoroughly the way one looks for a lost ring in a meadow. They didn't reach for a bigger piece farther away until they'd cleaned up all the crumbs before them. When the table was clean they moved on to the sideboard. The kitchen resounded with the music of feasting again. I knew that in the sideboard there was only a jar of marmalade, some sugar and a small bag of flour. The ladies consumed it all eagerly. Granny made little cakes of flour and marmalade, sprinkled them generously with sugar and fed them to her daughter. Herself, she ate them without sugar, protesting she didn't like them too sweet. When they got to the larder they were met with disappointment. The door was locked, the key hidden in an unknown place. I would have gladly gotten up and treated the old girls to all the food I had but was worried that catching them out on their greedy raid would embarrass them. So they stood hopelessly before the door examining the empty keyhole. Aunt Emilia threw in the towel first:

"Let's go, Mummy. I'm not hungry now, really … Those cakes were very filling … Mummy …"

With reluctance, Granny gave in, and both slipped out of the kitchen. I shuddered with disgust. The whole scene looked funny, even moving, when I was watching it, but now that the women were gone, I felt nothing but deep revulsion. I promised myself to send them away as soon as possible, on the earliest train, without sparing money or food for the road. I could not bear any more crawling around. I shut my eyes tight, pushed my head under the pillow and ordered myself to sleep.

I woke up early filled with determination to get rid of the old girls no matter what the cost. I heard a melody and the words of a church hymn. Granny and Aunt Emilia pottered around the kitchen singing:

"From the dawn
Our souls
Praise with song
Maaariiia …"

I lay quietly with my eyes shut. I felt snug and peaceful. I gently floated into the kingdom of childhood. Granny and Aunt Emilia pottering and singing. Daddy is not at home. Ah, how seldom I saw Daddy, and now Jurek, Juruś, Jureczek – he is in bed, napping. He is a child. His whole life before him. The whole world of unknown experiences, sensations and images, which were never to come to pass. The women stopped singing and began to confer in whispers. I opened my eyes and raised my head.

"Good morning!" I said almost cheerfully.

Still in my underwear, I entered the hallway. The bathroom door was open. The sheet covering the corpse was pulled half way off. If the women discovered my crime … I was unable to finish my the thought. I bent over the corpse. On the right side I noticed a shallow but wide wound, as if a bite had been taken out of it. There were other smaller wounds next to it, as well as scars and long scratches. It didn't look like the work of mice. I couldn't remember ever having had any in our house, anyway. The window was shut properly so entry from outside, by a cat or a bird, was out of the question. The pest must have already been inside the flat. For a while I stood still with my hand raised in a half gesture, totally lost as to what gesture it should be. I bent over the corpse again and put my hand under the sheet. When I took it out it was holding Granny's false teeth. So, it was the girls – having been turned away from the larder door, they had nibbled through the night at the cold rotting corpse. Poor things, they couldn't have had much of a meal. The flesh had been toughened by the ice. And getting it up from the bottom of the bath must have been hard work for them.

I stood turning over Granny's teeth mindlessly in my hand, unable to decide how to deal with this new situation. Did the old fogies know they were eating a corpse? Would it impair their weak health? Would they want to report me to the authorities? If they did, I would have to kill them without delay – but what would I do with two new corpses when I could hardly cope with the old one? So, the old corpse, again. It was clear that forgetting it was pure illusion. All these apparently unconnected incidents sooner or later led to trouble with the corpse. I could lock the bathroom door and pretend the whole thing never happened. But what to do with the teeth? Granny would certainly feel the loss of such a precious object very acutely.

At noon I escorted the women to the station. They said their good-byes affectionately, even effusively. I found them seats in a compartment and helped with the suit-cases. They left for starvation in a small mountain town. I gave them half of the money I had. I consoled myself with the thought that with their thriftiness it should last them a good few months. At any rate, I calculated that I still had a few months before the next wave of desperate letters, telegrams and then maybe another visit. By then Auntie's disappearance would be officially accounted for. The thought of this official explanation was very unpleas-ant for me and I kept pushing it to the back of my mind.

9

IN THE EVENING I MET WITH TERESA. IN A CORNER OF A
cheap café we sat talking, delighted and joyful. Then we
went for a long walk, wandering the streets. It was warm.
In the air one could feel the breath of coming spring. We
laughed a lot – at the lights in the puddles, the snowy
lampposts, fantastic silhouettes of old houses. Now and
again I brushed my lips lightly against my girlfriend's
cheek. We wandered into the cloister of a little old church.
It was empty. Below flowed a noisy, sparkling street. A red
light flashed at the crossing, tiny but clear. I thought, "red
elf," but didn't dare say it loud, afraid my voice would
sound harsh under the vast dome of the sky. Teresa knew
it and whispered into my ear:

"Penny for your thoughts?"

The red light disappeared and the outstretched gesture
of my hand toward the light was late and pointless. I embraced Teresa and we started kissing. For the first time we
felt the insufferable burden of clothes. We walked holding hands in silence, embarrassed by the fact that we still
hadn't become lovers. We both knew that a lively conversation now would be a fraud. When we came to Teresa's
house, she stopped.

"Go home, darling."

"I'll walk you to the gate."

"No, there's no need."

"Why?"

"I don't want ... You know what I mean."

"Is it embarrassing?"

"Of course not. But what's the point?"

It was the third time we were having this conversation. Nevertheless, we conducted it solemnly, repeating our lines without interrupting each other. The thought of going to bed alone, always an unpleasant one, today was simply terrifying.

"Yes, you are right, no point ..." I said slowly and bent to kiss Teresa's hand.

I headed home but when I looked back and saw Teresa's small figure disappearing in the distance I turned around and ran after her.

"Teresa," I said. "Teresa, come with me."

Without a word Teresa slipped her arm under mine and firmly took my hand. She was serious and calm. Feeling consecrated, almost canonized by our love and our decision, we got on the tram. Now and again, behind the rooftops, we saw the moon racing along. We were focused and silent. Only once, when I smiled at my girl, Teresa quickly put my hand to her lips. Our short journey along familiar streets, the elopement from a tram platform paid for with a discounted student fare, all that was so strangely beautiful I couldn't find any room to think or feel anything else but the thrill of flight filling my soul to the brim.

Only when we got off the tram did I begin to worry. The remains were well covered and I was not unduly worried that Teresa might discover them, even when she wanted to use the bathroom. I was more afraid that Teresa would start asking me questions usually asked by a new friend on their first visit, and force me to tell lies. Until now, when the conversation had drifted on to domestic arrangements, I'd offered some generalities and changed the subject. Teresa was too much in love and too happy to notice anything. Still, I remembered those petty lies and felt oddly distraught by them. Climbing the badly lit and dirty stairs filled us with cold. But finally ... we were alone.

We sat on the bed in the murky light of a small lamp. I looked for Teresa's hand. She leaned against my shoulder and lowered her head. She was waiting for a kiss. The seeming ease with which I could continue this simple game, the conducive atmosphere and the surroundings, began to make me feel uncomfortable. Teresa noticed it and became gentle and protective. I wanted to tell her to go away, that she couldn't even guess how I was deceiving her, but instead I kissed her. When our embraces grew longer and more ardent my fear and scruples receded. I surrendered to the caresses with the full inertia of my senses and will. Everything else, this whole bloody business, became so irrelevant and distant that talking about it now would have been simply rude.

I woke up early. Teresa was still asleep. The room was filled with the gray light of dawn. I sat up in bed and felt cold. We were both naked. The night, during which I was heroic and tender, lascivious and exalted, had passed. Teresa looked unattractive. Her mouth was open. I got up and walked to the bathroom to the sink. I took the mirror off the nail and looked at myself for long time. I cast a sweeping glance across the room, my eyes settling on Teresa. I burst into tears. My body was convulsed with sobbing. I tried to suppress it. I pressed my lips, rubbed the eyes – nothing helped. I poured water into the sink bowl and began splashing it over my face and shoulders, crying. I deliberately made a lot of noise, trying to drown out the sobs, while worrying I might wake up Teresa. But she slept soundly. At last I dried my face with a towel and began to dress, looking for my clothes and stifling the last spasms.

When I returned from the bathroom fully dressed, Teresa had already gotten up and put on her dress. I greeted her with a joyful smile. We exchanged a few words. Smoking my cigarette, I observed Teresa brushing her hair before the mirror. The morning dishevelment added to her charm. The beauty of youth, which needed no adorn-

ments, moved me deeply. Suddenly I was gripped by another attack of crying. Dressed, with shoes on, holding a
cigarette in my fingers, I threw myself on the bed, weep-
ing. The killing gave me my tears back. Teresa put away
the brush and crouched by my knees.

"What is it, love? What is it?"

I couldn't calm down. Wiping the tears away, I was
trying to take a puff of my cigarette, but with every attempt, more tears only fell on my sweater. Teresa sat next
to me and rocked my head in her arms. I was slowly calming down, listening to the gentle murmur of her words,
feeling the warmth of her hands on my face. I felt better.
I cried out all my tears, which I'd hoarded inside for all
those long years. And again I felt unable to cry. I pushed
Teresa gently away and sat opposite her.

"Listen," I began. "I've been meaning to tell you something, something I must tell you. I must, even if you will
hate me for it, or even destroy me." I noticed on her face
an expression of sympathetic understanding, which confused me. "I have to ask you first however," I continued in
a quiet, serious tone – "don't interrupt me. I want to tell
you this because I love you, and because I feel you are the
only person I want to tell it to."

Slowly, choosing my words carefully, I told her everything, starting with a broad sketch of my relationship with
Auntie and a discussion of the complex I had developed
about her, feeling totally dependent on her, despite being
younger and stronger ... The rest I limited to facts. I was
afraid I might lose my calm, raise my voice and begin to
gesticulate. But I managed to control myself and continued in an even, matter-of-fact tone of voice. When I finished, after a long moment of silence, Teresa asked me:

"Is that all you had to tell me?"

I nodded, but then immediately shook my head
vigorously.

"No, no ... I mean, don't worry, I don't have any more

sins to confess. But I'd like to tell you more, so much more ..." I mumbled.

Teresa got up and started putting her coat on. She walked past me as if I weren't there. Her indifference stunned me and got me shaking again.

"Teresa," I pleaded with her. "Say something ... You owe me an explanation, don't you think? What do you think about it ..." I stammered out hopelessly.

Teresa wasn't paying any attention. She seemed to focus her mind exclusively on simple things like closing her handbag and putting her kerchief on, the way I had when I lit the stove and prepared my first lonely breakfast. She started walking toward the door. I followed her and barred her way.

"Let me out," she said, "unless you are planning another ..." Her eyes were hard and fearless.

"Go then," I said slowly without moving. "Go, and later, after they've hanged me, you can boast to your girlfriends that you slept with a murderer."

Before I finished saying the last word she slapped me hard in the face.

"You have no right to hit me," I continued in the same tone. "If you want to, all you need to do is to say a word to those who can do it much better than you. No need to get offended. Sooner or later, you'll have to decide what you are going to do with this information. One can let go and forget all kinds of rubbish and trifles. But you – you cannot even forget the red elf."

The last words I said quietly and feebly. I didn't mean to be cynical. I had lost all my cynicism a long time ago. I carried on tired and dejected.

"That is why you have no reason to take offense. Perhaps it was churlish of me to say what I said, but you can't deny there was some truth to it. You are not, as far as I know, prudish or devoid of a sense of humor. Your attitude is of a woman who's open-minded and possesses a high dose of intelligence. And a touch of exaltation. All these traits indicate that you could be ... one day ... confided in ... not by everyone, of course ... but confided in quite lightheartedly ... you know ... with what I told you. I wouldn't blame you, just like I wouldn't blame anyone for anything, and not because I don't ... in my present situation ... have the right, but because I'm not convinced there is such a right. I think ... simply ... that we are all guilty."

Teresa knitted her eyebrows and listened.

"And you don't know, you simply don't know ..." I was beginning to lose the thread. "Telling you all this, I'm trying to spare you the ... so that ..." I completely lost it. "Teresa. Do you understand? Thousands of days, thousands of hours, during which nothing ever happens: the staple of my childhood and adolescence. Dreams that turn out to be just as empty. Or worse – they turn out to be a poison that kills any chance of healthy vegetation. Were we fed the stories of valiant kings, knights and other heroes – just to be vegetation? Why have I been condemned to vegetation? Who is to blame for it? Who?"

I began to pace the room. Talking gave me pleasure. Listening to the flow of my words, helping myself with gestures and seeing interest on Teresa's face, I felt, almost subconsciously, how much I loved myself. Humiliated and ridiculous, I abandoned myself, the crucified fool, to a desperate gesture. "I do not intend to justify my crime with the commonness of crime in our times. The fact that we all, day after day, gouge eyes, break arms and hearts, that we all hide corpses in our homes, does not excuse me from rightful punishment. We do not accept any other justice and the blindness of this one we know only too well. I do not mean to defend myself. If only because I do not feel guilty."

"It's terrible, but I understand you, and agree with you," said Teresa. "It's terrible."

"Today I could think that you need my help, you –
my red elf," I continued broodingly. "But that would be
misleading. I love you, Teresa, and our time together is
the brightest in my whole life. But beyond that? Do you
remember, darling, we talked about it – that it cannot last
forever? For ultimately, what choice do we have? Mar-
riage, legally sanctioned or not, or breaking up. And again
the torture of boredom. At least thanks to this bloody
business we still could be lovers."

Teresa frowned and asked, rather concerned now:

"Very well, but what can we do with it?"

"With what?" I asked confused.

"You know, with ... with Auntie."

"We'll clean it up somehow," I said absentmindedly,
and suddenly we both burst out laughing.

The exhilaration of the previous evening, the rapture
of last night, the despair of the morning and the horror of
the last hour – this whole concoction of moods exploded
with our young, healthy laughter. The solemn discussion
during which I'd put on professorial airs could not have
ended in any other way. We laughed like kids. Every time
we stopped and one of us tried to say something, it was
enough to look at each other and the intended words were
blown off our lips by laughter. At last, completely worn
out, we fell silent. Teresa looked at her watch.

"It's late. I have to go."

"Stay a bit longer."

"I can't. I'm famished."

"Excellent. We'll have breakfast in town."

"Excellent."

"You are a darling for not talking about home, where
they must be very worried about you now."

"I said I would stay the night at my friend's. And that
is how it was going to be, if you hadn't seduced this home-
less maid ..."

Laughing again we set off for town.

10

The honey days passed for us under the sign of the corpse. Going to the bathroom, Teresa dutifully ignored the bathtub with the chopped-up remains. I strictly forbade her to look under the sheet. Teresa was obedient. Her participation in the crime still had for her the charm of novelty. She devotedly followed the unwritten code of criminals. Her attitude toward me had changed into boundless adoration.

"I want to serve you, serve you," she would often say.

My attachment to her grew with every day. Every hour spent without Teresa was difficult. I could not imagine my life without our moments together, without our discussions, dreams and pleasures. When fear struck, Teresa brought me calm.

"My little one," she would say, stroking my hair. "My poor little one. Don't worry. Don't worry, I'm with you."

"Who are you?" I'd ask with my eyes closed, "Teresa?"

"I'm your girl. Your red elf."

"Red? Why red?" I would tease her.

"That's the color of the king of elves."

"Tell me about the king of elves."

Sometimes we would make plans for the future. Teresa, under the spell of our situation, believed everything was possible. We fixed the date of our escape and determined the picturesque routes of our travels. Those talks worked on me like opium. The reality of our situation seemed to me a trivial barrier, which could be blown out of our way with a puff.

On Sunday we decided to go for an excursion out of

town and drown two little parcels of the corpse in the river under the ice floes. At first I didn't agree to it.

"It's too risky, darling. It's my problem."

"I thought you've understood by now that problems aren't 'yours' or 'mine' – only 'ours,'" She answered contrarily. "And if not, too bad."

"But Teresa, you know the situation, I'm not hiding anything from you. I simply don't want us to go out on our first spring walk with such cumbersome baggage."

"It would be more cumbersome and unpleasant if you were to do it on your own. Isn't that so, my little one?"

"Yes, but do I have the right to put that burden on your shoulders?"

"It's like our baby. A consequence of me being with you."

On Sunday morning, some time after eleven, we got off a bus at the edge of a forest. Springtime and blue skies were all around us. The paths were dry but the fields shimmered under a spread of snow. We squinted our eyes against the sun.

"Isn't that parcel too heavy for you, darling?" I asked.

"No, my little one, it's not."

"Come on, let me carry it for you."

"Certainly not. You're carrying the heavier one anyway."

"That's ok, you are a woman. I should carry you in my arms – not make you carry parcels."

"The times we live in, eh?"

"You teaser, you," I laughed and put my arm around Teresa. She looked into my face, her eyes burning with fire.

"Ah, my little one, I'm so happy."

We put our parcels on the ground and began to kiss.

"Someone's coming," said Teresa suddenly. "Stop it."

We saw a man approaching slowly from the fields, carrying a gun. We picked up our parcels and walked on. The official cap of the forester reminded me of things I would rather forget today. Teresa noticed the change in my face.

"Why so sad, my little one?"

"Oh, it's nothing, nothing really," I replied, and then added sternly. "Don't look at the sun."

"Because?"

"Because you will damage your eyes, madame."

"What …? Ah, madame will damage her eyes … Oh, my little one …"

At the edge of the forest stood the yellow, ungainly building of the inn. We were the only customers there, except for a coachman in a padded work jacket drinking beer at the bar. Whenever I passed the inn before, the iron grille on its door was always shut. To this day it remains a mystery to me why it was open on that April Sunday. We sat down by the window, beyond which a panorama of the surrounding wooded hills spread out. We put our parcels on the empty chairs. After a while we were approached by a boy in a dirty apron and a face that was meant to show us we had disturbed his peace. After some protracted negotiations he agreed to bring us sausages and tea. We ate with an appetite of kids on a field trip, joking and laughing. When we finished our tea, we lit our cigarettes. The sky began to turn gray. Warmed and tired, we were looking at each other's faces and hands, which reminded us of our pleasures. We knew it was a beautiful moment. The gray mist clinging to the treetops invited a mood of longing and dreaming. So I began:

"You may not know it, darling, but my father lives in Buenos Aires."

"In Buenos Aires? And you never told me?"

"I'm telling you now. He lives in Buenos Aires and is a very rich man. The only problem is how to get there. Do you think it's impossible?"

"I don't know, love," said Teresa softly, "but since I met you nothing is impossible for me. Before I met you

I had never believed in any possibility of changing my fate. And to tell the truth, I never thought of it. But now, when I'm involved in such an extraordinary affair … It is extraordinary, isn't it, love? But maybe I'm hurting you, talking about it?"

I didn't reply. My eyes fixed on the horizon, I sat in silence, deeply moved and happy. Teresa's father was a forester and she spent her childhood and teenage years among the woods and lakes. Her first steps were blessed by the purity of nature, just as mine were cursed by neurosis. My longing for the forests and animals, stifled by years of misery, and forgotten in the recent days of the struggle with the corpse, now began to stir inside me uncomfortably. Many times I tried to see it in the cold light of reason, that it was all a question of love, that I should focus on happiness, for Teresa loved me too. Indeed I had many moments of true happiness, yet I could not free my mind from anguish. And it wouldn't be so bad if it weren't for the matter of my corpse. I knew that by hiding my feelings from Teresa I was deceiving her, and it hurt me. I could try and summon all my strength and remove the rest of the remains. But I had no strength left. Teresa competed with the corpse, and won. Over the last few days I hadn't undertaken any actions, only once slipping out at night with a small package wrapped in a newspaper and discarding the contents on a rubbish dump frequented by cats and crows. I felt burdened by the corpse like a man burdened with a family, of whose existence he doesn't dare to tell his mistress, while his inherent decency prevents him from shedding the burden. Even in the happiest moments, when walking with Teresa through empty fields, joyful and lighthearted, bursting with insuppressible laughter, so inextricably connected with our love, I carried the thought in my mind, which would suddenly flash like a signal – the corpse.

After a while I continued without looking at Teresa:

"I know a sea captain in Szczecin. A good man. When I was a child he used to carry me in his arms. An old, trusted family friend. I've learned he works now on a regular line to South America. Will you come with me?"

"Ah, Jerzy ..." Teresa stroked my hands with her fingertips.

Quietly, in low voices, we began to plot our escape. We refrained from showing any excitement in anticipation of all the exotic places we were going to see. No feverish discussions, no falling for the thrill of planning. We spoke in a calm, factual manner. I deliberately pointed out the difficulties piling up before us, while slyly slipping in suggestions of how to overcome them. Teresa pondered them, knitting her brow, returning her opinion in slow, measured words. When at last we reached a contented silence, she said:

"Sometimes, when you are not with me, I feel you do not exist at all. I'm sure that in a few hours I'll think this conversation is a dream. And yet you are real. I'm touching your skin and hair. My boy, my lover. You've put too much meaning into my life. Sometimes I feel it overwhelms me. But I know you cannot be any other way. I don't think I would love you otherwise, if you weren't full of all those mysteries I still know nothing about."

I squeezed Teresa's hand. She cheered me up. I felt like a good man. I gave a girl more than she expected. I made her happy the way I once made that old Capuchin priest in an empty church happy.

"Do you want to be with me?" I asked.

"I do."

We threw the parcels into the river from a high, overgrown bank. We didn't discuss their contents. Only on our way back through the woods did Teresa ask me, a little concerned:

"Darling, what was in my parcel?"

"Well, you know, surely ..."

"Yes, but ... which part?"

I remained silent.

"Come on, tell me. The leg?"

"Of course not, the leg would have been much heavier."

"I don't mean the whole leg ..."

"Teresa, stop it."

"You're right. I'm sorry."

She quickly lifted my hand to her lips. We sat down on a stack of logs in a clearing. Teresa took out two rolls and offered me one. Leaning on a log, I was contemplating the clouds drifting over the treetops.

"You know what, Elfie?"

"What, love?"

"Tomorrow I have national defense training again."

"Poor thing, I'm scared."

"Why?"

"I'm always scared before your training."

"Don't worry. It won't be for much longer now."

"What makes you think it won't be for much longer?"

"I'm sure of it, my little one. Before I met you, I didn't believe my life could change in any way. And I accepted that. In fact, it never bothered me much. But now, when I'm involved in such an extraordinary affair ... Just think, Jerzy, it's amazing ..." She fell silent and, after thinking for a while, she added with conviction: "I just know that everything will turn out as you want."

I waved my hand wearily. I knew that Teresa didn't really understand any of it. But her optimism and un-bounded faith in me began to disturb me. When we plotted our escape, planned our travels and other adventures, I usually put forward the most bizarre, fantastic ideas. I could even find logical arguments for them. And the down-to-earth, practical Teresa fell for my fanciful non-sense. As long as we believed in it together, it was all very nice. But now I was struck by what an enormous distance separated me from those moments. Did it mean I was bored with love? Probably not. I needed Teresa, I wouldn't want to lose her. Yet I realized with absolute clarity that the only real thing was the corpse, at once a millstone around my neck and my lifeline.

11

I checked the timetable and realized the better op-
tion would be to return by bus. Any other time I would
have been disappointed, but today the prospect almost
pleased me. I was disappointed by The Other Town. I
tried to shorten the wait for the departure by discovering
something special about buses. Unfortunately, I couldn't
find anything special. Their shape and yellow headlamps
just didn't fit into any metaphor. They were horrifying.
But only in their objective existence. I turned my eyes to
the station clock, hoping this poetic object might retain
something of the fairy tale I'd expected from The Other
Town. I looked at it intensely, lingering on the bright
little star at the top. Still, I felt I was losing my focus despite putting all my imagination and intelligence into the
effort. Suddenly I heard the characteristic blare of a horn
and at the same time, maybe just a few seconds before, a
young voice:

"Careful, mister!"

Someone yanked my arm. I let myself be pulled back.
A few inches before my eyes passed a bus. I turned around
towards my rescuer and recognized The Girl I Used to
See. Before I could get my bearings and get out of harm's
way, I stood in the middle of the road used by buses returning to the terminal. I had already grasped the meaning of this laconic message. Not for the first time The Girl
interrupted my most carefully laid plans of suicide, which
returned later only with double force.

I took my seat by the window and tried to adopt a position that would allow me to spend the long journey in the

best possible comfort. I focused my mind on that. As the driver switched the engine on, someone sat next to me. I turned my head automatically. It was The Girl I Used to See. I shuddered. I turned my head away and fixed my eyes on the window. This situation required some reaction on my part. I was trying to persuade myself that fate had graciously given me a chance. But then, I knew I couldn't take it, and felt rather ungrateful towards my fate. In the end I reached a compromise that best suited my mixed feelings: by observing The Girl I would destroy the myth of her Otherness, which in the meantime I had cultivated in my mind. Until now, almost always, I had seen her from a distance. Now that my face was practically next to hers, I would discover how common she really was.

I observed The Girl closely. Pretending to stare absent-mindedly through the window, I studied her reflection in the windowpane, her profile, her hands; I looked for signs of weariness in her face, which would make her just like the other passengers. After a while I could conclude with satisfaction that The Girl was tired; she even yawned once. And yet I felt defeated. The Girl still managed to retain the mystery of previous encounters. The distance I felt then did not diminish now, when our shoulders pressed against each other in the shared misery of fellow passengers. Her remoteness could be punctured only by talking to her directly. At first I thought of starting a casual conversation, in the course of which I would defeat her apparent unavailability. Except I wasn't really sure that victory would be mine. After all, talking to strangers had never been my forte. I cursed the situation forcing me into this. At that moment it was no longer just a question of destroying her myth but of wasting the chance – the chance I had already forfeited. I was not afraid of embarrassment. I was simply too lazy to undertake such a great effort. The thought of having an empty flat at my disposal disarmed me completely. And yet I was not ready to surrender. I could only console myself that in a couple of hours we would reach Our Town and The Girl would disappear around some street corner. That thought actually hurt. I counted the short stops bringing that moment inexorably closer. Suddenly I hear a loud crash and the bus ground to a halt.

The driver jumped out of his cabin and shouted something after a short while. Slowly, people started to leave the bus. I got moving too. The driver and the conductor were walking around the bus with their flashlights. It looked like something serious. Passengers complained and murmured among themselves. They looked like a lost herd of sheep; the sight cheered me up a little. We all stood by the roadside, close to the bus. Almost all the men lit cigarettes. I looked around thoughtlessly and suddenly saw a slender figure marching down the road with light, confident strides. It took me awhile to realize it was her. The Girl's movements were so strikingly different than the rest of the passengers, showing no sign of nervous impatience about the delay. It was hard to believe she belonged to the mass of commuters shuttling between the towns. The moon had just lit the road; there was no danger of me losing sight of her again. Some people began to walk around in small circles, as if locked in an invisible cage. Others took advantage of the bushes on both sides of the road.

I joined the walkers for a while and then broke away to follow The Girl. We left the bus far behind. The Girl marched on, her pace steady and purposeful, as if she knew exactly where she was going. We passed a wooden building, then a birch tree. The road began to rise. I expected that once The Girl reached the top of the hill she would turn around and start coming down. I stepped out of the shaft of light and over to the side. But she marched on. For a moment I lost sight of her. I hurried up a little. I was beginning to enjoy this. Suddenly I heard a roar. Its muffled sound confirmed we had covered quite a distance. Then another roar. After a while I heard the quiet purr of an engine. The Girl stopped and spread out her arms undecidedly. For a few seconds she stood still, as if struck by the moonlight. Then, slowly, she lowered her arms and just as undecidedly turned around. At first she walked slowly, like someone out for a stroll, then she broke into a run. I stepped out of the dark and walked toward her. As she passed me by I said:

"The bus is gone."

She stopped dead in her tracks. She looked at me carefully, without fear, and asked sharply:

"Who are you?"

"Ah … Mm…" I stammered. At first I wanted to say, "A murderer," for at that moment that was the most important thing about me. But I bit my tongue.

"A passenger," I said at last.

We began to walk slowly, following the direction in which our bus disappeared. We walked, picking up the pace, without looking at each other. The icy winter road, carrying us forward like a conveyor belt, the white downy fields, clusters of houses and lonely trees marked the rhythm of our march. The moonlight shone all the time. Now and again a hare skipped across the road. I was getting tired. The march, at first a relief from the murderous seat on the bus, was now beginning to turn into another type of torture. A slight nagging discomfort in my shoes and clothes grew sharper and more painful with every step. My feet began to slip. I stole a glance at my companion, wondering if she too had reached the point of exhaustion. But The Girl's clear face seemed just as untroubled as it was on the bus. I had no idea how far Our Town was, or whether it was at all possible to get there on foot. Several times I wanted to ask The Girl but I couldn't bring myself to do it, fearing that such questions were ridiculous in light of the merciless pace of our march, the road, the moonlight and the monotony of the landscape. When we passed the fourth village the road turned into the woods.

A grove of tall pines was quickly getting thicker, with more firs and naked deciduous trees. The moonlight began to disappear. I felt for The Girl's hand but found only the off-putting coarse sleeve of her coat and quickly withdrew my hand. Suddenly The Girl turned and, jumping over a ditch, stood on a high path wending among the firs. With some hesitation I followed. Seeing me undecided, The Girl beckoned and said:

"Come."

Or maybe she didn't say anything? We followed a slippery path, full of craters and roots. I watched my step but at some point I lost my balance and fell. The Girl stopped abruptly and when I quickly picked myself up, we moved on. At last we came to a small dell, all silvered and sheltered on all sides. The Girl turned to me and said:

"We'll rest here."

I didn't quite know how to behave in this situation. I looked around the dell and hesitantly fingered my coat buttons, wondering if I should take it off and spread it out somewhere on the snow. But The Girl started rummaging around in the low firs. Bent low, she swiftly ferretted under the brush like a small tornado. After a while she returned with an armful of branches.

"Help me," she said. "Here, hold this. Here ..."

Obediently I took hold of two sharp branches.

"Now here," ordered The Girl. "Good."

Soon I was working like a well-trained assistant, eagerly passing the prickly branches from hand to hand. The Girl did not slow down. She no longer spoke to me, only praised my diligence or criticized my sluggishness with an eyebrow or a grimace. Before long we had a thick mat. I don't know how long it took us to build our fir hut; at any rate I had to admit it was very warm and comfortable. Half-lying on the hard fir mattresses, we warmed up by the fire in the center of our camp. I raised my collar and stuck my hands inside my sleeves, worried that the warmth of the fire would prove illusory and the cold would start to bite. It was unnecessary. Our little house was getting warmer and warmer. Soon I was sweating like on a hot July day. Above the trees blew a sudden gust of wind. I could see thick trunks swaying a few feet away from our fire but here it was warm like in an overheated room.

The Girl took her coat off and her head scarf, yawned and began unlacing her boots. She got up and slipped them off without using her hands. I was surprised to notice that our hut, though very cozy, was nevertheless high enough for a grown woman to stand comfortably inside it. The Girl took off her trousers and sweater and lay down, wrapping herself in her coat. I looked at her in silence, swaddled in my winter coat with my raised collar and the lowered earflaps of my ski cap. The Girl wriggled for a while on her bed, then got up and moved closer. She took my face in her hands and suddenly kissed me on the mouth.

I stretched my arms out and embraced her. She started to pull away, laughing in a metallic, sinister way. Entangled in my coat, I couldn't decide if I should take off my gloves or my helmet-like hat, or hold tight to the trophy that was slipping out of my hands. The Girl helped me. She sat close to me and soothingly stroked my face and my hands. She took my gloves off and cradled the palm of my hand to her cheek. Then she let it slide off her knees, without letting it go. She brought her face close to mine and asked:

"Are you brave?"

"I am," I answered with conviction.

The Girl slowly raised my hand to her mouth and suddenly bit it. I grit my teeth. She held the bite with increasing force. I put my other arm around The Girl and started playing with her hair to divert my attention from the pain. She didn't react. At last she let go. I raised my wet, teeth-marked hand to my eyes. The Girl jumped up and fell onto her bed, wrapping herself tightly in her coat.

"Watch the fire," she called out, turned her back and almost instantly fell asleep.

I was hit by a wave of weariness too. With great effort I pulled up the sleeve of my coat to check the time. It was three in the morning. I thought of fighting sleep with a cigarette but the matches were wet and I had no strength to move closer to the fire. I just fixed my eyes on it with a firm resolve to stick it out like this till dawn. But The Girl's presence bothered me. I stretched my hand out and felt for her. I found a soft tress of hair and a cold smooth forehead. The Girl twitched and turned around. I felt embarrassed. Our agreement was that I was supposed to watch the fire. I turned my eyes back to the fire with renewed zeal. Another gale swept over the trees. Our little hut was getting warmer. I was boiling. Once more I tried to unbutton my coat but then gave up, suddenly worried I might catch a cold. I raised myself a little and immediately crumpled like a rag doll. My eyes shut automatically, against my will.

In the morning I was woken up by the intense cold, as if I had slept outside all night. I leaped to my feet. The Girl, dressed and ready to go, was smothering the fire with snow. All around us were scattered small, broken branches: the remnants, I suspected, of our little hut. I stood forlorn and cold. I felt ashamed, before the Girl, of my helplessness and lack of discipline in watching the fire. I didn't look great, I knew that. Without paying any attention to me, The Girl was trampling over the fire; then she bent down and threw handfuls of snow in my face.

"Catch me!" she cried cheerfully and ran off.

I started after her in hot pursuit. We ran among the

trees, knocking pillows of snow from the branches, and then ran down the road. At last The Girl stopped, looked at me, and burst out laughing.

"You fell asleep last night. The fire would have gone out if I hadn't woken up in time," she said. "But it's OK."

The last sentence she pronounced softly but firmly. I stretched out my arm automatically. She took my hand and pulled me after her. We walked fast through a silent misty wood.

"There is no point in looking for a bus," said The Girl. "My house is not far from here. I live outside the city. We'll go to my place and have a cup of tea. We should be there in an hour."

The wood began to grow thinner until it thinned out into groves, which I remembered from my own walks. Then on the horizon loomed the panorama of Our Town; we came out into an open space. Having passed a dirty village with huddled houses, still asleep, we turned onto a side road and after a while stopped before a big rusty gate. The Girl unhooked the chain and we entered a wildly overgrown, neglected park. Next to the gate, among the trees, stood a long yellow building, which looked like a warehouse or a coach house, but was empty. Farther on, along the alley, we came to some concrete foundations and empty swimming pools. Then again thick shrubs, almost completely covering the narrow path under our feet. Finally, we stopped before a barricade of empty, rusting cages. The heap of scrap was interlaced with tree branches; in the summer it must have created an impenetrable, iron-green fortification. The Girl pulled me again and we went inside a huge concrete tunnel, about six feet high.

After a few echoing steps we came out on the other side of the barricade. From the back it didn't look so fierce. Straight away my eye spied in the heap of creaky old iron a few weak spots through which one could easily sneak back onto the other side. We walked on among empty pens, cages and concrete ditches. When we passed a low hedge it was clear we were in a zoo. At first glance it didn't look much different from the junkyard we'd just passed. The animals sat inside their boxes, the floors of their cages covered with piles of snow. Only an old vulture flapped his wings in the nearest cage, and the black silhouette of a doe hovered above an iron fence. I remembered that I had once been in a zoo at this hour and wanted to tell The Girl, but as soon as I opened my mouth she shook her head sternly and silenced me. She took me by the hand and whispered into my ear:

"Come. I'll show you something."

I nodded, obediently refraining from saying anything. The Girl slowed down. We walked carefully and in silence; only her grip on my hand grew stronger. I couldn't understand why we were creeping like this, for that was the only way I could describe it, but I crept as best I could, holding my breath and trying to take steps without making any sound. When we got to a big hut, The Girl motioned me to hide behind a tree trunk. Leaning out from behind the tree, our faces were practically touching the wire fence of the cage.

Inside the cage, which was as huge as an auditorium, on a concrete shelf built into a massive rock, two lynxes were copulating. They did it softly, gracefully, soundlessly, without purring. It went on for an embarrassingly long time, and in silence. It began to get on my nerves. I felt I could not articulate any kind of reaction to this phenomenon, fundamentally indifferent to me and outside my direct sensual experience yet totally absorbing. I looked at The Girl. Her face was calm and beautiful as usual. She was watching it with concentration, her forehead slightly furrowed. Her lips were gently pursed in a kind of smirk, neither contemptuous nor ironic. The aroused animals began to moan and purr. It was unbearable. I tried to wrench myself free and cover my eyes with my hand. But

The Girl would not let go, her grip growing stronger still, her fingernails sinking into my hand. It was only thanks to my thick gloves that she didn't draw blood.

"Let go," I hissed with my throat tight. "Let go, now! I've had enough. This is ridiculous ..."

I was flailing madly behind the tree, unable to pull free. After a while I realized The Girl was no longer holding my hand; I was simply rooted to the spot. The lynxes' moans were growing louder and louder, reaching the pitch of beastly whining. I leaned against the other side of the trunk and with my eyes shut, waited out the feline orgasm. After another minute I decided to open my eyes. I was struck by the stillness of the surrounding. My writhing and flailing of a few moments ago seemed utterly out of place now as I stood in the midst of a silent snowy landscape. The lynxes lay on their bellies scratching each other lazily. The female lay with her hind legs stretched out like a woman's. A bird swayed a branch above my head and a single black leaf fell on the ground nearby. I turned around looking for The Girl but she wasn't there. I wanted to call her but remembered that I didn't even know her name. I walked around the cage, checking behind other trees; The Girl was gone. I became angry: What would be the point of looking for her anyway?

I checked the time. Ten o'clock. I decided to take the shortest route back to town. But as soon as I turned toward the alley I saw her, waiting for me.

12

THE FOLLOWING MORNING BEFORE DAWN I THREW MY SKIS over my shoulder and headed for the zoo. In fact, I hadn't arranged to meet The Girl but I was hurrying as if late for a date. The workers, gathered in groups at the bus stop, looked at me gravely, even hard-heartedly. I didn't have the time, or the patience, to explain to them that my needs, forcing me to take a ride to the woods at this time of day, were just as unforgiving as theirs, forcing them to hurry to the cigarette factory. After passing the bus stop I fastened the skis on and set off across the empty fields.

The gray skies made the snow glisten with a turbid sheen, which was hard on the eyes. The first part of the run, passing houses and cowsheds, was unpleasant, in fact, and now and again I asked myself if I shouldn't go back. How would I justify to The Girl such an early visit? Once inside the forest I began to enjoy the run, and the freedom. Sliding along the downy paths, past the black tangled mass of shrubs and bushes, here and there I would knock off a thick snowy hat from a fir branch, crying out in hushed excitement as I went along. I didn't let myself get carried away, constantly reminding myself I had to make it on time for the feline heat.

I entered the zoo through the main gate. I expected The Girl to be waiting for me there and was rather disappointed when she wasn't. I walked slowly along the alley. The animals watched me without any fear in their eyes. The bears stood up on their hind paws and had a closer look at me, but didn't turn their heads when I disappeared from their sight. A young lion ran away at first and then stopped with his paw in midair, above a still quivering wooden ball. I turned back and started toward the mouflon pen, behind which stood the caretaker's black hut. The hut looked as if someone had shoveled the snow in front of the gate, locked the door, bolted the shutters and left for somewhere far away. I stood before it for a long while, hesitating whether I should knock on the shutters or not, but in the end I lacked the courage. I turned back onto the main alley and began to move towards the other entrance, the one we had used. But I couldn't find the way. I had no idea which end of the park the lynx cage was at, which could serve as my orientation point.

Sliding along on my skis, I came across a long wooden building. Because I was feeling a bit cold, I unfastened the skis and went in through the half-open door. The inside of the building was like an elongated, over-wide corridor. Along the walls were cages with small parrots, hummingbirds and white-footed voles. The stench was overpowering. I lit a cigarette and moved towards the other end of the corridor, where I saw an open window. It didn't, as I expected, open up to the outside, but looked into a small room with a floor covered by layers of cotton wool and a small barred window that was closed. A big monkey in a black waistcoat sat in the middle of the floor. The animal held some kind of a magazine and was leafing through it with great concentration. After a while the monkey put away the magazine and pulled a sheaf of loose pages from his waistcoat pocket. I managed to catch a glance at the magazine's cover; it was an old satirical German weekly.

Meanwhile the monkey spread the pieces of paper out on the straw floor like someone dealing a game of Patience, except that the cards were uniformly blank. He fiddled with the glasses on his nose, though in fact there was just a wire frame without lenses, and sank into thought over his cards, as if trying to decide which to choose. Then, with a quick, thieving swipe, he snatched one of them from the middle row, moved to the window and raised it up to the light. As far as I could tell from that distance, the watermark on the paper was an erotic picture, drawn in a vulgar and naturalistic way. The monkey examined the paper at length, nodding his head with appreciation, then picked out another one and again looked at it for a long while. By the third card, the monkey's breast heaved with a soft sigh. He glanced at the fourth card quickly, as if not interested, and immediately reached greedily for the next. I had had enough.

I stamped my foot loudly and cried: "Shoo!" The monkey froze with a card in his hand, turning his eyes on me with a tense, painful look. Suddenly he leaped in the air, jumped on a ledge above the window and a metal curtain fell right in front of my nose. I began pummeling it, without thinking. Inside the room it was totally silent. From without, the parrots raised a deafening racket, their cries piercing my ears like steel shrapnel. The baboons and chimpanzees began thrashing about in their cages.

Tormented, I ran out of the building, slamming the door behind me. My skis were waiting for me in the snow, familiar and friendly. I fastened them on and threw myself into a run across the park. Suddenly, as I reached the main alley, the silence was rent by a hoarse, guttural shriek. I recognized the lynxes' call of love. Automatically, I turned in that direction. The noises grew more frequent; the intercourse must have been reaching the climax. I ran as fast as I could. At last, in the perspective of empty pens and barred enclosures, I saw the lynx cage. The Girl stood outside the caretaker's hut, pale, with eyes shut. Her face was somber, pained. I ran up to her and grabbed her in my arms. We fell on the snow. The Girl was kissing me feverishly and passionately, not possessively as before, but submissively, like a woman. The skis, still fastened to my feet, splayed widely, drawing long tangled spirals on the snow.

When we got up The Girl immediately returned to her previous role. She helped me wipe off the snow and in a dry, matter-of-fact tone, she observed that I was cold, and thus she invited me in for a cup tea. The caretaker's house was not abandoned, as I thought. We sat on the edge of a plush, richly tasseled sofa and drank our tea in silence. Apart from the sofa the room didn't contain any other furniture. The kitchen, however, was crammed with chairs, a long ungainly table and a sideboard.

"My father," said The Girl, "is of the opinion that I can receive guests only when the room is fully furnished. That is, when it has a table, armchairs, a linen cupboard and a clock. He thinks that now it would be improper to bring people in here. But I love you."

The Girl slurped her tea and we fell back into silence. I looked around the room and suddenly noticed a white piece of paper lying on the shiny floor, the same kind of paper the monkey had been looking at. I decided not to pay it any attention, but the paper seemed to fill the whole room and draw my eyes with magnetic force. I was trying to concentrate on her profile and her hands but my eyes, even when wholly focused on her figure, slipped down onto the floor and secretly sought out the accursed piece of paper. The Girl sat slumped, saying nothing and sipping her tea, of which she seemed to have prepared copious quantities for the two of us. I turned my eyes to the window but somehow the card still remained within my field of vision. The Girl lightly took my hand. I reciprocated with a gentle, though rather mechanical, squeeze. The presence of that card embarrassed me.

"Let's kiss," offered The Girl.

We began to kiss, but we were not enjoying it. Our kisses were cold and clumsy. I realized that The Girl simply had no idea how to kiss, as if she had never kissed in her life. We lay next to each other.

"We love each other," said The Girl indifferently.

"I love you and you love me," I confirmed, kissing her gently on the cheek. I fell into musing about our few common experiences. I told her about our little fir hut deep in the forest. The Girl listened quietly and when I fell silent she said:

"We built the little fir hut in five minutes. It's all nonsense. The little hut you were talking about is impossible, isn't it. My big, silly boy. You believed in a fir hut ..."

I wanted to protest but she calmed me down with a touch. The sound of a bell came from behind the window; with it came the sound of animals from all corners of the zoo. The Girl jumped off the sofa.

"Father is about to start feeding the animals. Come with me, you have to see this."

The Girl bent down and picked up the white card from the floor. She crumpled it quickly in her hand, then tore it into little shreds and threw it into the kitchen.

"I've had enough of this filth," she sighed. The bell whose ring had gotten us out of the empty room was affixed to the shaft of a cart, which was drawn by a donkey. A small man wrapped in a long black sheepskin and a big hat walked alongside the cart.

"We have a guest today," called The Girl. "I wanted to show him the feeding. You will start with the predators, won't you? Great. I knew the predators would be first."

The father didn't answer but The Girl kept talking, answering her own questions, laughing and teasing. The father stopped the cart in front of the low long shed and took out a basket filled with chopped-up meat and bones. His face was so swaddled in the collar, scarf and hat that I could not make out his features. They didn't seem to be that interesting anyway; his face was flat and unshaven. The father went back once more and brought out a second load of meat. When he came out for the third time he was carrying my auntie's corpse. From the first glance I had no doubt it was the very same corpse. Its limbs were cut off by the knees and elbows, the head chopped off with an axe. Father put the naked corpse on the cart and we moved on. The Girl squeezed my hand and whispered into my ear:

"We'll be feeding our cats, you know. Our wonderful lynxes."

I nodded my head and lightly brushed her head with my lips. We toured the whole zoo, stopping in front of the predators' cages. All that time I'd observed the naked torso trembling on the cart, making sure it indeed belonged to my murdered auntie. There seemed to be no doubt. The torso bore all the familiar marks: the signs of my victories and defeats, and on its side I even recognized the bite marks from Aunt Emilia and Granny. At last we got rid of all of the feed except for the corpse, which remained alone in the cart.

We were approaching the lynx cage. Despite a certain embarrassment, I felt joy. Now the nightmare of so many days was about to disappear down the lynxes' throats. I thought: here I was, accompanying my aunt on her final passage and I felt sorry that I might be saying goodbye to the corpse, to all that struggle, which had cost me so much effort and energy. Father, as if eavesdropping on my thoughts and hearing the word "funeral," took his hat off and followed the cart bareheaded. The Girl let go of my hand and lowered her head. Crows cawed among the treetops.

The lynxes, furry and excited, their eyes burning with a healthy appetite, crowded at the bars. Father raised the metal trap door at the bottom of the cage and slid in the torso. The animals began to eat. We watched how quickly and skillfully they dealt with the awkward body, how before our eyes the corpse was changing and losing its form. When the female ate her way through the side bearing the marks of my old girls' teeth, I sighed a sigh of relief. The corpse lost its attributes, was stripped of its personality. Finally, there was just a heap of bones of the floor of the cage. Father unbuttoned his sheepskin, pulled out a pack of cigarettes and offered me one. I looked into his eyes and recognized them; he winked at me discreetly. His waistcoat was red. The Girl cuddled up to me and put her arm around me.

We became a family.

13

AUNTIE RETURNED FROM THE SANATORIUM ALL WARM AND tan. She wrapped herself around my neck and kissed me on both cheeks. I felt a little awkward with her. I was at a loss how to explain the presence of her corpse in the bathtub, and then I was a little thrown by her new shawl and beret, the new buttons on her familiar coat. A long absence always creates that sort of distance. But Auntie was practical and good-natured, as usual.

"I haven't seen you for so long," she was speaking quickly, "how have you been getting on, my boy? I bet the flat is a dump, God have mercy on me. Why haven't you written? I was beginning to get worried, believe it or not. Have you been attending your lectures? I presume the place is just as I left it."

Weighed down by Auntie's bag I walked beside her, smiling. I didn't even try to answer any of her questions, knowing she wouldn't give me time to form a sentence. Auntie took me under my arm and chattered away.

"Shall we take a taxi? But I see they're all taken. We'll take a droshky, or let's go on foot. Such wonderful sunshine. Let's run."

Holding me fast by my arm she broke into a trot. She was running down the pavement, sweeping the passers-by out of her way. Auntie's heavy bag dragged me down, knocking about my knees. I was beginning to run out of breath. I watched Auntie's face, hoping it would soon be covered in sweat, and she would run out of breath too. Nothing of the sort. Auntie was trotting along, splashing mud with her boots. Apparently the sanatorium did her a lot of good. Before I knew it I was hanging off her arm, shuffling my feet just fast enough to keep my balance.

"How about some coffee?" Auntie screamed into my ear.

We were just approaching a coffee shop. I couldn't answer. I could hardly breathe and my eyes were watering. We burst into the coffee shop like a hurricane. Auntie ordered two coffees and two cakes. Munching forlornly on the cake, I listened to the outpouring of words from my auntie. There was no way I could get a word in edgewise or explain anything. At least I was pleased I didn't have to run with a heavy bag down a muddy street.

We covered the distance from the coffee shop to home at a more reasonable pace. Once inside, without taking her coat off, Auntie went into the bedroom and sat down heavily on the bed. Climbing up the stairs had taken some air out of her at last. Inside the four walls of our flat, I began to see the old signs of tiredness and age in her features once again. The moment of rest didn't last long, though. She got up, took off her coat and boots and began pottering about the flat. I didn't help her with her coat. At that point, my smallest gesture would have been irrelevant and meaningless before the decisive, impending moment. I sprawled on the bed, listening to Auntie clattering around in the kitchen. I was waiting.

At last the door to the bathroom squeaked. I got up. I couldn't resist participating in the most dramatic moment of the whole adventure. Auntie stood over the bath, shaking her head.

"Boy, boy, boy," she said with reproach, "why did you bring all these plants in here? And how could you clutter the whole bathtub like this? I bet you didn't take a single bath while I was away, did you, you dirty boy. Help me move these plants."

With some reluctance I began to shift the old araucaria while Auntie picked up the two cacti and we took them back to the room. My little altar ceased to exist. The scraps of the corpse littering the bathtub among the ice were cold and devoid of any charisma. Auntie clutched at her head.

"Jerzy," she cried, "what have you been doing here? Get the brush, let's clean it quickly. Pull up your sleeves, you'll get your shirt dirty."

I got down to cleaning the bathtub. The torso presented the biggest problem. Though gutted, it was still quite heavy. But Auntie helped me. We carried it onto the kitchen balcony and hung it out on the balustrade.

Just then, on the neighboring balcony, Mrs. Malinowska was beating her carpets. Seeing Auntie, she sent her a radiant smile and the two ladies exchanged pleasantries. I took the last remains outside in a bucket and chucked them into the rubbish bin.

Auntie poured half a packet of cleaning powder into the bathtub and, armed with brushes, we started scrubbing it clean.

GUYS LIKE ME BY DOMINIQUE FABRE

Dominique Fabre, born in Paris and a life-long resident of the city, exposes the shadowy, anonymous lives of many who inhabit the French capital. In this quiet, subdued tale, a middle-aged office worker, divorced and alienated from his only son, meets up with two childhood friends who are similarly adrift. He's looking for a second act to his mournful life, seeking the harbor of love and a true connection with his son. Set in palpably real Paris streets that feel miles away from the City of Light, a stirring novel of regret and absence, yet not without a glimmer of hope.

I CALLED HIM NECKTIE BY MILENA MICHIKO FLAŠAR

Twenty-year-old Taguchi Hiro has spent the last two years of his life living as a hikikomori—a shut-in who never leaves his room and has no human interaction—in his parents' home in Tokyo. As Hiro tentatively decides to reenter the world, he spends his days observing life from a park bench. Gradually he makes friends with Ohara Tetsu, a salaryman who has lost his job. The two discover in their sadness a common bond. This beautiful novel is moving, unforgettable and full of surprises.

WHO IS MARTHA? BY MARJANA GAPONENKO

In this rollicking novel, 96-year-old ornithologist Luka Levadski foregoes treatment for lung cancer and moves from Ukraine to Vienna to make a grand exit in a luxury suite at the Hotel Imperial. He reflects on his past while indulging in Viennese cakes and savoring music in a gilded concert hall. Levadski was born in 1914, the same year that Martha—the last of the now-extinct passenger pigeons—died. Levadski himself has an acute sense of being the last of a species. This gloriously written tale mixes piquant wit with lofty musings about life, friendship, aging and death.

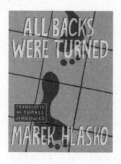

ALL BACKS WERE TURNED BY MAREK HLASKO

Two desperate friends—on the edge of the law—travel to the southern Israeli city of Eilat to find work. There, Dov Ben Dov, the handsome native Israeli with a reputation for causing trouble, and Israel, his sidekick, stay with Ben Dov's younger brother, Little Dov, who has enough trouble of his own. Local toughs are encroaching on Little Dov's business, and he enlists his older brother to drive them away. It doesn't help that a beautiful German widow is rooming next door. A story of passion, deception, violence and betrayal, conveyed in hardboiled prose reminiscent of Hammett and Chandler.

ALEXANDRIAN SUMMER BY YITZHAK GORMEZANO GOREN

This is the story of two Jewish families living their frenzied last days in the doomed cosmopolitan social whirl of Alexandria just before fleeing Egypt for Israel in 1951. The conventions of the Egyptian upper-middle class are laid bare in this dazzling novel, which exposes sexual hypocrisies and portrays a vanished polyglot world of horse-racing, seaside promenades and nightclubs.

COCAINE BY PITIGRILLI

Paris in the 1920s—dizzy and decadent. Where a young man can make a fortune with his wits ... unless he is led into temptation. Cocaine's dandified hero, Tito Arnaudi, invents lurid scandals and gruesome deaths, and sells these stories to the newspapers. But his own life becomes even more outrageous when he acquires three demanding mistresses. Elegant, witty and wicked, Pitigrilli's classic novel was first published in Italian in 1921 and retains its venom even today.

SOME DAY BY SHEMI ZARHIN

On the shores of Israel's Sea of Galilee lies the city of Tiberias, a place bursting with sexuality and longing for love. The air is saturated with smells of cooking and passion. *Some Day* is a gripping family saga, a sensual and emotional feast that plays out over decades. This is an enchanting tale about tragic fates that disrupt families and break our hearts. Zarhin's hypnotic writing renders a painfully delicious vision of individual lives behind Israel's larger national story.

THE MISSING YEAR OF JUAN SALVATIERRA BY PEDRO MAIRAL

At the age of nine, Juan Salvatierra became mute following a horse riding accident. At twenty, he began secretly painting a series of canvases on which he detailed six decades of life in his village on Argentina's frontier with Uruguay. After his death, his sons return to deal with their inheritance: a shed packed with rolls over two miles long. But an essential roll is missing. A search ensues that illuminates links between art and life, with past family secrets casting their shadows on the present.

THE GOOD LIFE ELSEWHERE BY VLADIMIR LORCHENKOV

The very funny—and very sad—story of a group of villagers and their tragicomic efforts to emigrate from Europe's most impoverished nation to Italy for work. An Orthodox priest is deserted by his wife for an art-dealing atheist; a mechanic redesigns his tractor for travel by air and sea; and thousands of villagers take to the road on a modern-day religious crusade to make it to the Italian Promised Land. A country where 25 percent of its population works abroad, remittances make up nearly 40 percent of GDP and alcohol consumption per capita is the world's highest – Moldova surely has its problems. But as Lorchenkov vividly shows, it's also a country whose residents don't give up easily.

Killing the Second Dog by Marek Hlasko

Two down-and-out Polish con men living in Israel in the 1950s scam an American widow visiting the country. Robert, who masterminds the scheme, and Jacob, who acts it out, are tough, desperate men, exiled from their native land and adrift in the hot, nasty underworld of Tel Aviv. Robert arranges for Jacob to run into the widow who has enough trouble with her young son to keep her occupied all day. What follows is a story of romance, deception, cruelty and shame. Hlasko's writing combines brutal realism with smoky, hard-boiled dialogue, in a bleak world where violence is the norm and love is often only an act.

Fanny von Arnstein: Daughter of the Enlightenment by Hilde Spiel

In 1776 Fanny von Arnstein, the daughter of the Jewish master of the royal mint in Berlin, came to Vienna as an 18-year-old bride. She married a financier to the Austro-Hungarian imperial court, and hosted an ever more splendid salon which attracted luminaries of the day. Spiel's elegantly written and carefully researched biography provides a vivid portrait of a passionate woman who advocated for the rights of Jews, and illuminates a central era in European cultural and social history.

 New Vessel Press

To purchase these titles and for more information please visit
newvesselpress.com.